ACTION-PACKED APARTMENTS!

NOVELLAS BY
FRANK CONNIFF

Published By
Podhouse 90 Press
ISBN: 978-0-578-97947-2

First Edition, 2021

Design, Typesetting and Cover Design by Len Peralta

THE CRAZY CAT LADY
IN APARTMENT 2B
PAGE 5

THE TRUE CRIME PODCASTER
IN APARTMENT 3C
PAGE 75

THE CRAZY CAT LADY IN APARTMENT 2D!

1

Not long ago, I started spying on my neighbor. It wasn't a high tech surveillance operation like you'd see in a Jason Bourne movie or anything like that. It was more traditional, mostly involving me looking through the peephole into the hallway outside my door that separated our apartments.

Does this old school method of spying make me seem retro in a cool sort of way?

No, it doesn't, does it? I'm just coming off as creepy.

I am aware that as the protagonist in this story, it's not a good idea to let you in on such a disturbing fact about me right off the bat. I've written a great many online posts about how the three Star Wars prequels are all hampered by confusing storytelling that doesn't give us a hero to clearly identify with and root for.

The rooting interest for me hasn't quite kicked in yet, has it?

But the story I'm telling here is not fantasy, it really happened to me, and it wouldn't have gotten underway in the first place had I not become fascinated by the mysterious actions of my neighbor across the hall. Trying to get a glimpse of her through my peephole is what started this whole thing off. So I guess you could call me an anti-hero. In fact, please do call me an anti-hero because that would be a lot more polite than some of the other things you could be calling me.

Look, maybe a rooting interest in a protagonist isn't as important as I thought it was. For my sake I sure hope it isn't.

I live in an apartment building on the Upper East Side of Manhattan. It's one of the quieter neighborhoods in the city. Not a lot of partying goes on, and you don't hear much noise-making, unless one of the many senior residents in my building is having a heart attack, but those parties tend to end early.

I'm sixteen, so I don't really fit in with many of my neighbors, but to be honest, I don't fit in with kids my own age, either. There are some guys I talk about movies and TV shows with, but they aren't as knowledgeable as I am; they don't do the deep dives into filmographies and mythologies that I do. They don't watch as much or read as much as I do; they go outside and socialize and even play sports. They've managed to find many activities that are somehow more enjoyable to them than having awkward, stilted conversations with me, if you can believe that.

I might be a bit old for my age but that doesn't mean I don't look my age, I've got UPS-package-brown hair that screams, "super cuts" and a body with baby fat that refuses to grow up and leave the nest. But I think I have what they call an "old soul," which is supposed to be an inner thing but it somehow got splattered all over my face.

Not that I relate to the old folks in my building. I think some of them resent me for being so dull so young. They worked long and hard to become the boring people they are and they see me as an upstart who hasn't earned his tediousness.

It occurs to me that it also might not be a good idea to start this story by telling you how unexciting I am. But on the other hand, now that I've already presented myself as a creepy peeping weirdo, my credentials as a sympathetic, relatable hero have already gone by the wayside. But please bear with me while I give you a few more quick details about my life. (Better to get the backstory over with now than devote a whole trilogy of prequels to it, right?)

I live with my older brother, who is twenty four. My dad had a stroke so my parents moved to Arizona, I guess because, well, why not? For a man with my dad's coronary issues, it makes sense to move to a place where the pastrami isn't as good.

In the interest of not disrupting my school year my parents entrusted my sort-of-adult brother to take care of me, and they even paid the rent on this two bedroom apartment for us to live in. My brother would prefer to live downtown in the Village, or Brooklyn, but living rent free anywhere in New York City is something you can't put a price on.

My brother spends most of his time at his girlfriend's apartment in Williamsburg. Jake is an awesome guy and we get along, but I cramp his style. I think cramping someone else's style is probably the only style I have.

So yeah, my neighborhood is boring, my building is boring, and my neighbors are boring. Except for one. The object of my fascination: the crazy cat lady who lives across the hall in apartment 2D.

What's the fascination? Well, I had never seen her and I knew nothing about her. I only knew she was some crazy lady with a lot of cats. Her name wasn't listed on her mailbox. She never checked the mail because that would have meant leaving her apartment and she never left her apartment. I figured she was old and couldn't make the walk, or maybe she didn't want to be separated from her cats.

Nobody knew how many cats she had, but estimates among other tenants in the laundry room that I eves-dropped on ranged from a dozen to between fifty and a hundred. I always thought this was an exaggeration because if she had that many, I think I would have smelled them, but the odor coming from her apartment was no different from the stale odor coming from every other apartment. The whole building has the musty stench of life after it's already been lived, and her apartment seemed no different.

I did hear an occasional meow coming from behind her door and that was enough for me to believe she was a crazy cat lady because...why not? I was bored and in the market for things to think about.

I guess for the purpose of this story I should build up the suspense about how many cats she had but I'm just going to tell you right now she had four. That's it. Sure, four is kind of a lot, but it's not an insane amount of cats to have, especially if you're a crazy cat lady. I'm glad I didn't find out the truth when I was speculating about her because I needed my imagination to do the work that real life was not capable of.

What little I knew about her, like for instance that she was a crazy cat lady and not a crazy cat man, came about because the only time her door opened was when delivery men arrived with takeout orders of food. I would look through my peephole to watch these exchanges. It was prime time appointment programming for me. Seeing cartons filled with General Tso's Chicken or soaked bags of French fries or boxes of pizza or whatever she was having for breakfast, lunch or dinner was my one insight into her world of intrigue. I only barely saw her hand taking the food; she stuck it out and grabbed the bags so quickly it was like she had been trained in the ancient art of agora-ninja-phobia. But when I heard one delivery guy say, "thank you, miss," another say, "thank you, ma'am," and still another say, "thanks, lady," I deduced she was a woman. Pretty nifty detective work, huh?

She never, and I mean, never, left her apartment. I figured it was probably frailty, a fear of breaking her hip. Believe me, I had been around these old people in this neighborhood for so long I was afraid I was going to break *my* hip.

Still, anytime I heard a knock on her door, I dropped whatever video game I was playing, TV show I was watching, or book I was reading, and ran to the peephole. Seeing food delivered to her door had become my favorite form of entertainment, although it wasn't the kind of entertainment, like the Marvel Cinematic Universe, or a Netflix series, that I could post and pontificate about on Twitter or Reddit. I had yet to differentiate between how one episode of food delivery was a better watch than another food delivery, and I couldn't analyze how one take-out arrival fit into the oeuvre of a particular delivery guy who was proving himself to be a Grub Hub auteur, so I couldn't give this viewing experience the deep dive that I gave to TV shows and movies.

One day during my regularly scheduled peek through my peephole, the usual routine was disrupted, and this is where the action and adventure begins so maybe I should have started the story at this point instead of wallowing in the Phantom Menace opening crawl that is my regular life.

There was a delivery man at the crazy cat lady's door, but even though I could only make out the back of his head, I could see that a big burley guy had a knife to his throat. This didn't seem like a policy the local sushi place would enact. And there was also one other big burley guy standing next to him on one side of the door, and two other big burley guys standing on the other side of the door. They all had hard, gravelly faces and matching black suits that would be appropriate at a funeral, especially because the men wearing the suits looked like they were responsible for a lot of funerals.

This looked like some kind of ambush to me, maybe some new form of aggressive elderly euthanasia.

It was sinister, no doubt about it. My conscience — such as it is — was telling me I had to do something. So I stood at my peephole and continued watching. I quickly realized this hardly qualified as doing something, and if tragedy happened and I didn't take any action, I would have to live with it for the rest of my life.

I decided to live with it for the rest of my life.

But then I coughed. Since my nose was right up against the door, the big burly guys all heard me, and they all turned and stared at my peephole.

I panicked. I knew they knew I was staring at them.

Without thinking, I swung open my door and said, "does anybody have a lozenge?"

I immediately realized how stupid that was and slammed the door shut, making things about a million times worse for me.

Looking through the peephole again, I saw the four burley dudes move menacingly towards my apartment, but then the crazy cat lady's door swung open. A hand reached out and pulled one of the burley guys into the apartment. The three other guys turned and rushed in after him, and the door slammed shut behind them.

The delivery guy dropped his bag of food on the floor and ran like hell out of there. I think he had come to accept that he wasn't getting a tip.

I kept my eye on the peephole. Observing something and not participating in it was what I was good at and I was determined to stick with my strengths.

I heard banging and grunting noises coming from the crazy cat lady's apartment. There was hitting and crashing and objects being broken, with a few cat meows and hisses thrown in.

I took out my cell phone to call 911, so the police could come and save her and save the cats and maybe save my frightened ass while they were at it. But I was so nervous I dropped the phone to the floor. I was trying to be a good neighbor and failing miserably.

I bent down to pick up the the phone and by the time I got back up and looked through the peephole, the need for emergency police assistance had passed. The crazy cat lady's front door swung open and the four burley men fell out of the apartment and onto the hallway floor, as if they were being ejected by the strongest bouncer in the world. This was some serious Dalton/Pain Don't Hurt/Best Cooler In The Business/I Thought You'd Be Bigger/Road House-level stuff going on.

Then the door slammed shut behind them.

The big burley guys all lay on the floor bloody and covered in bruises. One of them had a broken arm. Another had a serious head injury. The other two had bloody noses and scratched up faces. They were all moaning loudly, in considerable pain. Thank God.

I kept as silent as I could. I was afraid they might bust through my door and kick my ass, just so they could end their outing with at least one easy victory. But they staggered down the hall and headed for the exit. Their main priority now was to get immediate medical attention, the kind that involves lots and lots of morphine.

Continuing to look through the peephole, because that had become my thing, I noticed that the food delivery bag was still on the hallway floor.

Suddenly the door burst open and the crazy cat lady stepped out into the hallway and grabbed her order of food off the floor. As far as I knew it was the furthest she had ever been out of her apartment.

She looked nothing like I thought she'd look. She wasn't what you'd expect from a crazy old cat lady. For one thing, she wasn't old. Her hair was dirty blonde, long and messy, and it covered a lot of her face, but she looked like she was maybe in her late twenties/early thirties. What I could see of her face was pale and cosmetics-free. I didn't quite make out the color of her eyes because she was squinting; I don't think she saw much sunlight or much of any kind of light. She wore a Ramones t shirt and black leggings. For someone who never went outside she appeared to be in excellent shape.

But the most striking thing about her was that she didn't appear to have a single cut or bruise. Even without the battle to the death that had clearly happened, it would be miraculous to have those four big burley guys in your tiny efficiency apartment and still avoid injury. But apparently she did. Wow.

No, she was not some incapacitated old lady. If I had happened to see her in the elevator, I would have immediately considered her the coolest person in the building, which, granted, is a low bar.

This might be my one chance to meet her. If had come across her in any other normal setting, I would have been too frightened to say one word to her, because I'm usually too frightened of real life human interaction to say anything to anyone.

But this felt like an extraordinary circumstance, so I was compelled to do something amazing:

I opened my door and blurted out, "are you okay?"

Not exactly a clever opening line, but honestly, I was genuinely wondering if she was okay.

She shot me an intense, indifferent stare. I thought she was going to say something nasty, or more likely, not say anything at all, but instead, with no expression on her face or in her voice, she said, "I'm fine, thank you."

She clutched her bag of food and returned to her apartment.

Before the door shut, I got a glimpse of four pairs of eyes staring at me. Her cats.

I had not only seen the crazy cat lady, I had seen the crazy cat lady's cats.

Pretty exciting stuff, huh? Can anything possibly top that?

For God's sake, let's hope so.

For several days after that I didn't see her or hear anything coming from her apartment, and if something had happened, believe me, I would have known, because what I had witnessed with those nasty guys getting their asses kicked made me more obsessed than ever. Seeing her in person did nothing to diminish her mysterious allure. She was spending a lot of time living rent-free inside my head while I sat living rent-free in my apartment. Say what you will about the fantasy life I built around her — it was affordable.

There was the occasional food delivery to her door but I only got the usual glimpse of her hand sticking out and grabbing the bags. I hate to admit it, but food delivery without violence is just not that interesting.

There also might have been a few deliveries I missed; I still went to school, and during those rare times when my brother was home, I had to pretend to be interested when he talked about his life, as if working downtown and hanging out with his buddies and having sex with his girlfriend could possibly be more fascinating than my solitary existence of listening at the door and staring through the peephole. If his life wasn't so much better than mine, I would have felt sorry for him.

My brother was supposed to be looking after me and making sure I didn't get into trouble, but he took note of my apartment-bound life and figured I was the least likely kid to ever get in trouble. I could have pointed out that I had created some explosive controversies on social media with my incendiary posts about the shortcomings of certain Zack Snyder films, and how I had totally decimated another online poster who went by the handle Eradicator 1 when I kept calling him Ejaculator 1 and it pissed him off to the point where he sent me several angry emojis. But I didn't want my brother to worry about me.

The truth is, my strong online presence meant an even stronger presence within the confines of our apartment, leaving my brother free to roam the city and do whatever he wanted, secure in the knowledge that I was being kept safe by the most dependable babysitter in the world: my personality.

My brother had somehow inherited a self-confidence gene that bypassed me entirely. I mean, sure, I was downright cocky and self-assured when addressing anonymous avatars in cyber settings, but not so much if humans revealed themselves to me in their brick and mortar forms.

Anyway, I can't remember specifically what I was brooding over that afternoon when I was coming home from school, about to put the key in my lock, when I heard the door behind me open slightly.

I turned around. The crazy cat lady, still standing within the confides of her apartment, but clearly visible, said, "Hey."

"Hey," I replied. (I felt bad that I had ripped off her conversation starter but I couldn't think of anything else to say.)

She leaned forward and stuck her head out just far enough to glance up and down the hallway, but I got the impression that it wasn't another round of deadly assassins she was afraid of, it seemed more like it was the mundane aspects of everyday life she was on guard against.

"Could you come into my place for a second? I need to ask you something," she said.

I was both excited and frightened. Human interaction frightens me under the most normal of circumstances, but in this case I might be interacting with a cold-blooded serial killer in need of teenage blood for her nightly satanic ritual. Still, even if that was the case, becoming a human sacrifice would have been the most interesting thing to happen to me in a long time, so I decided to accept her invitation.

In the moment that I was hesitating, her leg was shaking anxiously, and she shot me a look that seemed to say, "come on, decide already."

So maybe she wasn't a serial killer, maybe she was just conventionally neurotic. The thought of this disappointed me slightly. I guess I was hoping for someone who was broken by life in a bigger than life way.

She led me into her apartment, immediately shutting the door once we entered. It was a small studio with a standard-issue tiny NYC kitchen. It looked like she had just moved in, even though I knew she had been a resident for a few years. But there was nothing on the walls, and just one ratty couch, a coffee table with a Mac laptop and a universal remote surrounded by food stains, one floor-to-ceiling bookcase with mostly hardcover books, and a 51 inch flat screen TV that dominated the apartment. This was a woman who never went outside so it was a good bet that a lot of reading, binge-watching, and maybe even binge-eating went on here, although there was a small alcove with weights and exercise equipment, so apparently she kept herself in shape for her walks from the couch to the kitchen to the front door and back.

It's misleading to say there was very little furniture. I mean human furniture. There was plenty of cat furniture. Lot of things for the cats to sit on: cat beds, scratching posts, a climbing tower, and cat toys strewn about the room. This was a place where cats were relentlessly cared for, and the cats all gazed at me with uniformly emotionless looks that gave you the impression they all had a deep capacity for ingratitude.

"Have a seat," my host said.

"We haven't formally met," I said. "My name is Wallace." Introducing myself seemed a smart gambit. It could possibly give the false impression, at least for a few seconds, that I was actually capable of conversation.

"I'm crazy cat lady," she replied.

"What do your friends call you?"

"I don't have any friends."

"Well," I said. "You have enemies. I saw that for myself. What do they call you?"

"They're usually not conscious long enough to call me anything. But you can call me Lydia."

"Is that a code name of some sort?"

"It's my name."

"Oh. Okay. Cool code name."

Great. I was already coming off like an idiot. As you can see, once introductions are done with, my conversational skills tend to fall apart.

I sat down on her couch. It was the only place to sit not meant for cats, but you could tell by the rips in the fabric and layers of hair that they had laid claim to it many times.

Lydia sat next to me. I was probably the first non-assassin visitor she'd had in a long time, maybe ever. But she looked comfortable as she sat. The further into the apartment we got, the more relaxed she was. Whatever self confidence she possessed was completely square footage-based.

It wasn't a big couch, so we were pretty close to each other. I won't tell you how fast my heart was beating, but if any of the many AARP members who lived in the building had a heart going at this rate, an ambulance would have been called.

"I wanted to thank you for helping me out the other day," she said. "I mean, you didn't help me out one bit, you might have even been a hindrance, but still, you didn't call the cops and I appreciate it. The last thing I wanted was the police involved. Your lack of civic engagement is something I deeply appreciate."

"Thank you," I said. "I'm glad my bad citizenship is finally being recognized."

It felt like a stupid thing to say, but then again maybe it was a funny thing to say. I wasn't sure. I was going to let her decide, because if my sixteen years of life had taught me anything, it's that my value and worth are based on the judgements of other people.

She stared at me. She took a moment to decide if she wanted to smile or not, then after weighing the pros and cons, she smiled.

"You're kind of a wiseass, aren't you?" she said. "I suspected you might be. I had an instinct about you."

"Really? What?"

"That you're a typical modern teenager who uses snark to cut himself off from any real emotion, but you also seem like someone I can trust. My instincts about people are usually right."

"What do you do to cut yourself off from genuine emotion?" I asked.

"Oh, lots of things," she said, warming to the subject. "I stay indoors, avoiding human contact, and when I do come in contact, I often inflict severe bodily harm, and that's a great way to avoid true human feelings. In fact, after I've kicked someone's ass, I usually feel nothing. The way other people self-medicate with food, I do by beating the crap out of bad guys. Not that I don't also love food."

Okay, now she was scaring me. I looked at her cats, as if they'd give me some support, but they were as disinterested as ever.

She noted that I was looking at her cats, and she said, "my cats are my best friends. They're as fond of not leaving the apartment as I am."

We were silent for a moment. She noticed the awkward look on my face, and then said, "You think it's sad that my cats are my best friends, don't you?"

I didn't know what to say, but before I could say anything, she said, "who are your best friends?"

This question stumped me. I thought for a moment and said, "Um...your cats?"

This time she smiled without hesitating. "I knew I was going to like you. Can I ask a favor?"

I was tempted to say yes without even hearing what the favor was, but I kept my cool. Something told me that she was about to involve me in something monumental.

"I need you to look after my cats," she said.

Okay, monumental is not the right word. This was not something I could easily brag about to other kids I wanted to impress: "Yeah, that's right, I've been getting into cat sitting lately, pretty cool, huh?"

"So, you're going to leave the apartment?" I said.

"Yes," she said. Then she sighed and settled back into the couch, as if hoping the cushions would engulf her.

"It's been a while since I ventured out," she said. "But some people are after me, and I need to talk to a certain person to find out more info, and he insists that I talk to him in person. Can you imagine that in this day and age: preferring one-on-one contact over texting or tweeting or zooming? What a pain."

"But won't leaving the apartment mess up your life as a crazy cat lady who never leaves her apartment?"

"Exactly! But this is the only guy who can give me the information I need. He knows this, so he's insisting that I come to him in person."

She stared off into space for a moment, looking distressed. It was like she wasn't afraid of anything, yet also afraid of everything.

"So do you want the cat sitting job?" she said.

"Let me think about it. Yes."

"I can pay you a hundred dollars," she said.

"Wow!" I said. "That seems ridiculously generous, probably way too much." Then, I added, "I'm not very good at contract negotiation, am I?"

"Well, the thing is. I'm not sure how long I'll need you here," she said. "It might just be a couple hours, or it may take an eternity. Or, I might run right back into the apartment two seconds after I leave. But I'll pay you the same no matter what."

"You didn't seem too afraid of those big dudes who were trying to harm you. Why are you afraid of leaving your apartment?" I asked.

"It's a long story," she said. "About five years ago, my brain was broken. I think the passage of time has healed it somewhat, but I'm not sure if it's fixed. I've always known I would have to get out of the house eventually, but leaving the cats alone worried me. Then when I saw you the other day, I thought to myself, 'here is a guy who looks like he's got nothing going on in his life, so I bet he's just the one to look after my cats."

"You do have good instincts about people," I said.

She smiled again, but I noticed that even when she smiled, there was anguish visible on her face.

And I had my own worries. "Are those big burly dudes going to come back?" I said.

"No," she replied. "The guy that I'm visiting assured me that if I came to him, no one else would come here."

That was a relief. I'm shy around people in general, and deadly assassins in particular.

So now I wondered if I was capable of facing what could be the greatest challenge of my life: looking after her cats.

Then I had to face the even greater challenge of facing the sad fact that looking after her cats was the greatest challenge of my life.

Well, whatever the case, she had just hired herself a cat sitter.

Lydia stood up, and I thought she was going to leave, but then she sat back down. She had suddenly found an excuse to not leave the apartment and she seemed relieved.

"Oh, there's something I forgot to tell you," she said.

"About what?"

"My cats. You know, I was allergic to cats until I met them. They are wonderful. But there are some things you need to know."

She pointed at an orange tabby that was sitting on top of the climbing post. Judging from her lethargic expression, it was hard to believe this cat ever walked, much less climbed up to the perch.

"That's Hayley," she said. "She's sweet, but don't ever look directly at her."

"Why not?"

"She'll force you into a staring contest, and that's not something you ever want to do, believe me."

"I won't. I'm no good at staring contests, or any kind of sports."

She gestured towards an older long haired black cat seated on one of the bookshelves.

"That's Duke. Just leave him alone, don't touch him, or interact with him, and he'll leave you alone. It's his way of showing affection."

"Got it," I said. (I didn't get it.)

"If you do bother him, he will erase your mind. It's temporary, but on the other hand, there's been no research on the long term effects of kitty mind erasure. So, seriously, leave him alone."

I've never had a cat. My mother didn't like them and my brother thinks they're uncool, so I had no experience with them. Still, I didn't see how a house pet could erase a person's mind, even temporarily. Seems like that would be something they should tell you about at the shelter before you adopted one, right?

Not that it mattered in this case. I saw that Duke's eyes were almost but not quite completely closed. A mutual leave-each-other-alone-society between us seemed like an easy thing to achieve.

Lydia then directed my attention to a gray-haired cat that was snugly curled up in a cat bed.

"That's Jerry. Do not, I repeat, DO NOT let him him scratch *anything* except the scratching post."

"There's not a lot here for him to scratch," I said, surveying the sparsely furnished space she called home.

"Don't let him scratch anything. His claws are capable of tearing a hole in the fabric of our universe, and that's a mess you don't want to have to clean up."

I couldn't help myself, I had to comment on this:

"I think I'm finally beginning to understand the 'crazy' part of 'crazy cat lady.'"

I expected her to be offended but she wasn't. She just became more earnest. "I'm telling you, when Jerry scratches fabric or the wall, or anything other than his scratching post, demons emerge that will burrow into the very core of your soul. It's not something you can always see, but believe me, you can feel it. You end up confronting things floating up from deep inside yourself that you'd rather not confront."

"Can't you spray him with water or something when that happens?" I said.

She was not amused. Her expression was stoic and grim. But she wasn't mad at me, either. "Look," she said. "I thought I had a good instinct about you. I picked up a vibe that you're a person who can handle weird information. There are things beyond our everyday perception that would terrify you if you got a good look at them. I've seen a few things, believe me."

She starred off into space for a moment, kind of the way a cat would. "I really don't want to leave this apartment," she said.

"Does this mean I'm being laid off as a cat sitter?"

"No. I have to leave. A lot is at stake. Circumstances are compelling me to overcome my fondness for inertia."

I was about to ask her exactly what was at stake, but then she pointed at a slightly overweight white fluffy cat sitting in the middle of the floor and staring at us, following our conversation like a tennis match.

"That's Edna. If I'm not back soon enough you'll have to feed her. When you do, you're going to need this."

She pulled out an armored shield from behind the couch. It was like something you'd see in a King Arthur movie, or at least one where the Knights of the Round Table carry police riot gear (that sounds like a pretty cool movie now that I think of it).

"Make sure you are shielding yourself with this when you open a can of cat food and pour it in her bowl. I mean it, you're going to need the protection."

Well, at least the idea of a cat attacking someone was a concept that took place in the material world we all live in. It was the closest thing to non-weird behavior of her cats, not that it wasn't still pretty weird.

I looked at her, then I looked at the cats. They were all in a state of contemplation, gazing off into some distant land only they could see. That was normal enough, but I got the impression that Lydia thought she could see into their world as well.

"Couldn't you have just gotten a hamster?" I said.

She laughed. "Not a bad idea."

Now that I had made her laugh, I felt like I would do anything for her. Yes, I am that needy, but I had never met a crazy cat lady before and it seemed like I had been missing out. It's a shame that we never have much of a chance to talk to shut-ins, because the fact that they're shut-ins makes it logistically hard to converse with them. But I bet the thing that makes a person a shut-in — the trauma that caused someone to never want to leave their homes — is a big part of what makes them interesting in the first place. If they only understood how being alienated from the human race made them fascinating, they'd be the life of the party.

"Now that I've filled you in, I'm going to go on my trip," she said. She handed me a remote control device.

"Here, this will make your cat sitting more interesting," she said. "I have the most awesome lineup of TV channels you've ever seen. It goes beyond what's available on normal systems. Only certain people are allowed to view it, and while I'm not exactly allowed to view it, I do have access to it."

"How?"

"Let's just say I have my ways."

"Were you part of some secret government agency or something?"

"You've watched a lot of movies and TV shows, haven't you? Well, now you're going to get a chance to watch even more."

"You haven't answered my question."

She turned towards the door. She had no intention of answering.

"Help yourself to whatever is in the fridge," she said. "There's lots of leftover take-out food. Some of it has been there for a while and might give you botulism, but no worries, the kitties will be able to feast on your decaying flesh for months if I don't come back right away. Anyway, see you soon. I hope."

She walked over and opened her front door. Then she closed it again. She turned back towards me, but then she turned around and opened the door again.

"I can do this," she said. "I can do this."

She walked out into the hallway. She looked to her left, then looked to her right. Then she turned around and faced me. It was everything she could do to not walk back into the apartment, but instead she took a deep breath without opening her mouth. She closed the door. I heard her footsteps in the hallway, but then I heard nothing. Then a few more footsteps, then nothing. This pattern repeated itself a few times, but then the footsteps became a distant sound and then disappeared altogether. I thought I might hear her come running back, but I didn't, so after a few minutes it was clear she had left the building.

I gave all four cats a look, as if to say, can you explain this woman to me? But I had only been there for a few moments so I wasn't ready to get my Doctor Doolittle on and start having conversations with animals yet. Maybe it was the cats themselves who turned people into crazy cat ladies, so I would have to be on my guard and not let them suck me into their furry vortex. I'd have to make a point of only engaging in small talk with them and not get into any substantive discussions, and oh my God, maybe it was happening to me already!

I would focus on my job: looking after them. They seemed fine, content to just sit and stare off into space. They looked like they could drift off to sleep at any moment. So knowing they were alright, I turned my attention to a more pressing matter: Lydia's TV.

Was it really the awesome channel lineup she said it was? In my apartment we only had basic cable and a couple of streaming services, so I was curious to open my eyes to a whole new world of human experience, the kind that can only be achieved alone in a room with no physical contact.

I picked up the remote and turned on the TV.

"Mr. President, I've obtained the files you've been waiting for," a man was saying directly to the camera. I immediately recognized him as the Secretary of Defense. This didn't appear to be a regular TV show, it looked like a top secret briefing being transmitted to the White House.

The Secretary of Defense then looked at a different camera angle and said, "We'll be right back after this."

Or maybe it is a TV show. But then an old actor whom I recognized as Tom Selleck came on the screen and said. "A reminder: any unauthorized person watching this will be subject to a lifetime in federal prison, or possibly death, which means you'll never grow old enough to qualify for a reverse mortgage, which is a wonderful option for senior home owners." Then he smiled and added, "Now back to our top secret briefing."

Some might say I instantly changed the channel because I feared federal prosecution, but honestly this didn't look like a very good show. The pacing was sluggish and the production values were low.

But I was glad I did change the channel because I next came across a new movie with Keanu Reeves as John Wick doing battle with Joaquin Phoenix as the Joker. But the word "new" didn't really do it justice because this was a film that was just an online rumor. In other words, this premium cable channel was so premium, it aired films that hadn't even been made!

Holy crap, this really was an awesome channel lineup!

I watched the rest of the movie, which was a bit disappointing. I love John Wick films, but I vehemently hated Joker so much I only watched it five or six times. But this movie seemed rushed and underdeveloped, which made sense since they might not have even started filming it yet.

Then I flipped through the channels, and came across a few more top secret government briefings, which I quickly turned away from. Then I saw what looked like a public access show from somebody's home. There was a gnarly looking dude sitting in a throne of a chair, surrounded by floor-to-ceiling shelves of action figures from every movie and TV show you could think of, all in their original packaging. I couldn't decide what was more pathetic, that a grown man owned so many toys, or that I envied him for owning so many toys. I was about to turn the channel when I saw a woman enter his lair that I immediately recognized as Lydia.

So the person she was visiting had a broadcast channel on this weird top secret cable system? I wondered if Lydia knew this. I was about to call her on the cell phone number she left, but I decided I wanted to watch and listen in on their conversation first. I had begun my career as an eavesdropper by merely peeking though my peephole; now I was taking my desire to hear stuff that wasn't any of my business to the next level.

"Okay, you dragged me all the way to your sad home," Lydia said to the guy. "I endured the stress of the streets, and the subway, now I need information."

She sat down and blew the hair out of her face. It had taken her less than an hour to get there but she looked like she had been through a perilous journey. I know it seems this way to a lot of New Yorkers going about their daily business, but she looked like she was taking the grind of getting from one place to another in New York City harder than most.

"Why the hostile attitude?" the dweller of the sad home said. "If I had told anyone at the agency you were coming here, you'd be dead already. But I didn't, isn't that cool?"

"How did the agency find out where I live?" she said. "I've had five years of peace and quiet, and now this. What happened?"

"I made finding you a personal project of mine," he replied. "I know how much you love General Tso's Chicken, so I hacked into the computers of every Chinese Restaurant in New York and did a system analysis of apartment addresses that ordered that dish the most."

"And that's how you figured it out?"

"Yeah, I mean, a few poor souls who love General Tso's Chicken got their heads bashed in, but we got to you eventually."

"Speaking of heads getting bashed in," Lydia said, moving menacingly towards him. "Seems like your thick head is long overdue."

"Wait, hold it," he said. "You're not being fair. Everything I do, I do on your behalf. You're the whole reason I joined the agency in the first place. I have an all-consuming love for you and I'm willing to destroy the lives of anyone and anything that blocks my path. You don't think that's sweet?"

You could tell from the expression on Lydia's face that she did not think it was sweet. Not at all.

"I'm just a romantic at heart," he said. "I have this vision of the two us, arm-in-arm, snuggled up together on a couch, watching the world burn."

She grabbed his lapels.

"Tell me what's going on?" she said. "Tell me what you and the agency are up to!"

"Okay, okay!" he said. "What's going on is..."

He then looked at the camera and said, "Oh, crap, I forgot that my premium cable channel is broadcasting right now."

He hit a switch and then the screen went dark.

Damn, just as I was starting to get into it! Oh well. I flipped the channels and watched more programming that was rare and never before seen by the general public: The Magnificent Ambersons with the ending originally filmed by Orson Wells, the entirety of the Back To The Future trilogy, but with Eric Stoltz starring in all three films instead of Michael J. Fox, some movie called Bogart Slept Here with Robert De Niro, and some other film called A Glimpse of Tiger with Elliott Gould, plus The Day The Clown Cried with Jerry Lewis, which I immediately flipped away from, not because it was forbidden but because it looked like it probably should have been.

I was settling in to watch Tim Burton's Superman Reborn with Nicholas Cage when there was a knock at the door.

Well, not so much a knock as the front door being busted down.

Four big burley dudes swept into the room. Big burley dudes showing up at this place was becoming a trend around here, but last time Lydia was present to do whatever it was she did, but now it was just me and the cats.

Lydia had assured me this wasn't going to happen, and I was mad because now I was going to miss a lot of the Tim Burton movie, but on second thought I was probably going to miss all of it because the TV channel line-up at the Intensive Care Unit is probably not nearly as good, and I bet they don't even have any cable whatsoever at the morgue.

IV

These four big burley guys were different from the four big burley guys who previously visited the apartment. They had more of a professional paramilitary thing going on. Dressed in black, carrying machine guns, wearing ammunition like jewelry, they kind of looked like ninjas who had decided halfway through their training that, you know what, screw the ninja thing, let's just get assault weapons and shoot people.

I had a feeling they weren't there to bust me for watching illegal cable, but I knew I was in deep trouble, the kind of trouble that might result in me leaving the building in a body bag, not an unprecedented event considering the demographic layout of my neighbors, but something I was hoping wouldn't happen to me for another seventy years or so.

"We've come for the cats," Blonde Vin Diesel said.

(Strangely enough, in the midst of all this stress, I still had the presence of mind to give names to these guys I had never met. I was learning that even in the throes of imminent danger, I was capable of thinking extremely pointless thoughts.)

"Don't make a move," Eurotrash Tucker Carlson said.

It probably won't surprise you to hear that I didn't make a move.

"We're taking the cats," another guy said, one I hadn't named yet. "If you stay out of our way I promise we'll kill you quickly."

This was not comforting to me in the least. It was all I could do to not faint. Odd that I was in a roomful of cats and I was going to be the first one to take a nap.

The guy I hadn't come up with a name for yet gave Hayley, the orange tabby sitting on top of the scratching post, a menacing stare. Hayley returned his stare with a look that no human could ever match in terms of intensity. It was the kind of look you'd see if you ever saw one of the children of the corn taking an eye exam.

The unnamed dude looked back at her. He couldn't stop looking. He tried to turn away, but couldn't. It was the grand master tournament of staring contests.

"Cobra! Look away!" one of the other guys said.

Cobra? Seriously? That was his name? I had just decided to name him Stocky McConaughey, but I had missed my chance to get in on the ground floor of naming him.

His head looked like it was about to explode. Finally, with great effort, Cobra, aka Stocky McConaughey, turned his head away and released his eyes from Hayley's gaze.

This unleashed a hurricane gust in the apartment. A bunch of paper-weights and hardcover books, including The Power Broker by Robert Moses, and Infinite Jest by David Foster Wallace, flew off of Lydia's book-shelves and hit Cobra/Stocky McConaughey in the head. He fell uncon-scious to the floor.

Hayley now had a look of smug satisfaction on her face. She had made all this happen with her kitty mind. The bad guys knew this. These cats had certain powers. If all they could do was eat, sleep and defecate, like most cats, there'd be no need to dress up in paramilitary gear to come get them.

"Grab the cats before they do anything else," Baby Face Rambo said. (Ad-mittedly I wasn't trying too hard, but that's what I named him.)

He said, "I'll take care of you first" to Duke, the long haired black cat, who was sitting closest to him, on the bookshelf.

Duke then wiggled his head, as if shaking a spray of water from his face, and this had an instant effect on Baby Rambo's mental state.

"Where am I?" he said, looking around the room in confusion. "Who am I? What does it all mean?"

This must have been the mind-erasure that Lydia told me Duke was capa-ble of.

Small-Boned Stallone (my Baby Face Rambo revision, admittedly no better) dropped to his knees in terror, as if the Angel of Death, wearing a hockey mask, had entered the apartment.

"What's the point?" he cried. "Nothing exists. I don't exist. There is only nothingness, Nothing. Nothing."

Well, for someone who didn't exist, he was certainly taking up a lot of space. He looked like he was about to cry. He was now way too emotional-ly distraught to do the vicious thug thing.

There were two functioning bad guys left, which was still two more functioning bad guys than I was capable of handling.

"Enough of this nonsense," Blonde ponytailed Vin Diesel said. (I had just noticed this detail about his hair so I added it to his name.)

At that moment, Jerry, the gray haired cat, started scratching the couch.

"Oh, crap," I said. "He's not allowed to scratch anything except the scratching post."

I didn't think the bad guys would care about this, but oddly enough, Blonde Ponytailed Vin Diesel did. He became fixated on the balls of cotton that oozed out of the couch. Then his eyes moved from the rips in the couch to the air above the couch. He stared intensely into that empty space with a look of sheer terror.

Now he acted as if some sort of invisible demon was engulfing him.

"No! No!" he yelled. "The faces of those I've wronged have emerged from the couch and are rising to haunt me! Stay away! Stay away!"

He screamed in anguish, then fell to the floor and balled himself into the fetal position. From that moment forward he cried like a baby, but a baby whose psyche had been seared by an existential dread that engulfed his soul like a severe diaper rash.

He was also like a baby in that he wet himself. Any hope he might have had that he was going to come off as cool was severely diminished by the stench of pee-pee, although at least his urine was fresh and up to date, unlike his 1980s-era ponytail.

There was now only one bad guy left, but he was still big and menacing and still had a machine gun, so that was more than enough to keep me just as scared as before.

"Maybe you're the one making the cats do these things," Eurotrash Tucker Carlson said, pointing his gun directly at me. "So I'm going to finish you right now."

"I assure you I have no influence over these cats," I said, my voice shaking. "They don't even like me. I swear, I'm the last person they'd ever take psychic instructions from!"

I was about to go full John-Turturro-in-Miller's-Crossing and beg for my life with complete abandon, but I backed into the kitchen and knocked into the electric can opener, setting it off.

The moment that sound filled the air, Edna, the slightly overweight white fluffy cat, leaped from the floor. She bounced off the wall, onto the guy's head, and then onto the counter where the can opener sound had come from.

The guy was disoriented for a moment but then he got his bearings and pointed the uzi right at me.

"You're dead," he said.

What he meant was that I was about to be dead. Seemed like a high price to pay for looking after a neighbor's cats, and it was beginning to dawn on me that these cats were more than capable of taking care of themselves, which only made my impending death seem all the more pointless.

He started to squeeze the trigger, but then a coffee mug with the words, CATS MAKE PURRRFECT PETS hit him in the head and he stumbled. The back of his head hit the wall, and then he fell unconscious to the floor (bad guys falling to the floor had been happening in this apartment a lot lately).

Lydia came into view and stood over the fallen bodies.

"Well, it's good to be back in the comfort and safety of my apartment," she said.

"Yeah, welcome home," I said. "Have you met the killer assassins you said were never going to come here?"

Lydia looked down at the defeated bad guys like a slightly annoyed mom who wanted her kids to pick up their room. "Okay, out of here, all of you, now!" she said.

She collected their weapons — guns, grenades, ammo, everything. "These are mine now," she said.

(Well, there weren't all hers. I discretely picked up an oval object with a label that said "smoke bomb" on it and shoved it in my pocket. I wasn't planning to do any harm with it, I thought maybe I could use it at school to get out of doing a test or something like that.)

The bad guys staggered out of the apartment with no protest. It wasn't said out loud, but it was more than implied that they had to go think about what they did.

"And how was your day?" I said.

"Stressful as hell," she said. "But now that I'm back, I'm glad I went out-side. It was a big step for me. But I'm really sorry about what you just went through, although I knew that if something like this happened, my cats would protect you."

This seemed like an absurd thing to say, but then I remembered: uh, she's right, that's exactly what happened.

"I've lived here for five years without anyone visiting me except food delivery people," she said. "Now it's like an open house for assassins here."

She reached into her pocket and pulled out a wad of bills. "Here's the hundred bucks I owe you."

"Since those cats are so good at taking care of themselves, why did you even need a cat sitter?" I asked.

"To feed them, silly," she said.

"Don't I get combat pay?"

"What combat did you do? It was the cats who did all the fighting."

"Fighting? What I saw wasn't fighting. It was more along the lines of...I don't know...sorcery?"

"Pets are marvelous, aren't they?"

"There is a way you can pay me extra for what I went through."

"How?"

"Tell me what the hell is going on around here!"

She thought about this for a moment, sighed a little, then said, "Okay, fair enough. I'm hesitant to tell people about the true nature of my situation, but I think I can tell you without worrying about other people finding out."

"Because I'm so trustworthy?"

"No, because you don't appear to have any friends."

She had me there.

"I'm starving," she said. "Let's order some takeout."

She thought for a moment, then added, "Oh, crap, I'm out of cash. Wait! You've got money. I guess you're buying."

About a half hour later we were sitting on her couch with several contain-ers of Chinese food spread before us on the coffee table. She ordered from an expensive place, got a lot of food, and gave the delivery guy a big tip. She was very generous with my money.

"Okay, here's what happened," she said. She placed an iPad on the arm of the couch, then resumed eating, saying nothing for over a minute.

"Well?" I finally said.

"Look," she replied. "I don't like to talk while I'm eating. This whole thing started when I was recruited by a covert government agency. The iPad has the top secret report about what happened. Reading it will tell you everything. It's forbidden for any civilian to see such highly classified material, you could be arrested for treason just for looking at it, but hey, knock yourself out, and try not to get any hoisin sauce on the screen."

Here's what the document said, word for highly classified word:

REPORT FROM DAVID ST DAVID, EXECUTIVE IN CHARGE OF RESEARCH, RECRUITMENT, AND DEVELOPMENT, A.I.A.I.A. (AMERICAN INDY-ALT-INTELLIGENCE AGENCY):

The following is an update on the status of our recruitment of new personnel in the fields of intelligence, espionage, and covert warfare. It all started with an employee review of the waitstaff at Wild Bill Donavan's, our restaurant in midtown Manhattan. As you know, this dining establishment is owned and operated by the American Indy-Alt Intelligence Agency. Everyone who works there as a waiter or bartender wants to to be a covert government operative, or a secret agent, or a combat commando. It's no different from any other New York City restaurant, where waiters and waitresses aspire to be actors or singers or dancers. But we hire people who want to work in espionage.

We picked one of the staff members as a good prospect to promote from waitress to commando-in-training.

The waitress we chose is named Lydia Rollins, and she seems perfect for our needs. She's pretty, and has other skills that might be helpful, like athletic ability and physical coordination. She's also quite smart, but we believe we can work around that.

She was of course excited for the promotion, but as often happens in cases like this, her fellow aspiring secret agents who worked on the waitstaff were resentful and jealous. One eager young man named Lance complained that he was more experienced and worked dinner shifts during the busiest nights of the week and therefore was more qualified to go on top secret overseas missions. When I pointed out that he had once gotten my order wrong, bringing me chicken wings with chipotle sauce, rather than barbecue sauce, he claimed that was a false flag operation, but I didn't believe him. His negative attitude was uncalled for, so if we weren't short-handed we might have assassinated him, but let's wait till after we see how busy this weekend's brunch is before we make a final decision.

Agent-in-training Lydia Rollins signed the necessary paperwork and showed up early the next morning for our extreme physical training program.

It turns out our instincts about her were right. Her training continued for several months, until eventually she became the kind of lean mean killing machine that embodies America at its finest.

Needless to say, she was excited when told we felt she was ready for her first mission.

But she was a bit taken aback when presented with her uniform. It was a head-to-toe black unitard with strategically placed pockets and holsters for weapons and ammunition. She said she was expecting a more traditional camouflage outfit but we told her those were out of fashion now and what she was wearing was the latest paramilitary design from Paris.

We told her there was a warehouse near the Brooklyn waterfront teeming with a heavily armed sleeper cell of dangerous terrorists. Her mission was to neutralize them, but not kill them, as they would be needed later for torturing, I mean, questioning.

Agent Rollins was not aware that as she entered the warehouse and proceeded with her mission, we observed her every move through hidden surveillance. It wasn't long before she came across a half dozen large men wearing masks and body armor and brandishing assault weapons. She executed her training adroitly, disarming and judo kicking some, karate chopping others, and battling them all with remarkable skill. She was one of the best fighting commandos any of us had ever seen, and the fact that she was still basically a trainee and thus drawing a comparatively small beginners salary made it all the more satisfying.

But she was maybe too good. She managed to kick one of her adversaries so hard he crashed though the two way mirror we had installed.

She saw that there were several movie theater-style seats set up with about a half dozen or so young men who had been watching her in action through the two-way mirror. Some were out of shape and slovenly, others were pasty, thin, and sunlight-deprived. In other words, these were young male computer geniuses from all over the country. We were trying to recruit them to work at our agency. They were the whole reason for this demonstration; in fact, they were the whole reason Agent Rollins had been promoted to commando, but *she didn't know this yet.*

"What's going on here?" she demanded. The young men were quickly rushed out of the room, but not before one of them, perhaps the most promising recruit of all, Evan Overman, turned to her and said, "That was so cool!"

The fact that he was inspired and more than a little aroused by Agent Rollins' demonstration was all the proof we needed that this operation was headed towards success. She was not yet aware that impressing and enticing these brilliant young men was the whole point of her employment at the agency.

But she did suspect something was amiss. When I emerged from the observation room, carrying a clipboard and ready to compliment her on what I deemed an excellent performance, she demanded to know what was going on. I didn't want to tell her, I wanted to do something productive like knock her out and deprogram her, but unfortunately I left my taser in my other pants, and anyone in the near vicinity who could have shot her had already been knocked out by her.

I realized that the nature of this operation was such that telling her the truth was a bad option, but then I decided that getting seriously injured by her was an even worse option. I had to weigh the national security consequences of my divulging secrets against the consequences of the stressed-based bowel movement I was about to drop in my pants, so under the circumstance I think any reasonable person can understand why at that moment I sang like an American Idol contestant.

I told her that the entire reason we had promoted her to commando was so she could help us attract young male computer nerds into the organization. Her combination of physical attractiveness, along with her natural athletic ability, and her combat skills, were quite enticing to technologically-inclined young men who grew up watching sexy female action heroes in movies, TV shows, and violent video games. These brilliant geeks had lucrative careers in Silicon Valley for the asking, so how were we, with our comparatively limited tax payer dependent budget, supposed to attract these techno-geniuses? The answer was making them think that if they came to work for us, they'd be surrounded by real-life equivalents of Buffy the Vampire Slayer, Lara Kroft, Black Widow, Aeon Flux, Ultra Violet, and Wonder Woman.

"So, I'm only here to be objectified?" she said.

"Yes," I replied. "But on behalf of your country. I need you to understand that being a fantasy figure to developmentally stunted young men is your patriotic duty."

You'd have thought this reasonable explanation would have altered her thinking, but you'd be wrong. She just didn't love her country enough to let her body be exploited.

"So you're not going to send me on a real mission? she said.

"Of course we are!" I said. "You just need to understand that all of your missions will involve stimulating the testicular regions of male computer geeks."

I might have expected an emotional response from a woman, but I was taken aback my her anger and the threatening look on her face, so I observed protocol and went ahead and crapped my pants.

This proved to be a canny strategy on my part. Her attitude changed, a look of resignation came over her, and she sighed as she said, "well, I guess it still beats waitressing."

She stepped back a bit, and in what I took to be a conciliatory tone, said, "did you just shit your pants?"

I told her that that information was highly classified and on a strictly need to know basis, and I considered disciplining her for her insubordination, although maybe the fact that she had to smell my load was discipline enough; however, when I saw that Evan Overman enthusiastically signed up after watching her in action, I realized I had been right about her potential value to our organization. She remained with the agency and resumed her daily workout and training regimen, and she stayed alert and seemed to accept that at a moments notice, she would be enlisted to serve the masturbatory needs of her nation.

VI

At this point I became uncomfortable by what I was reading. It seemed wrong to think of this woman that I had been daydreaming about for months before I had even met her as some sort of fantasy figure. I looked up from the report and said, "This is all very interesting, but it doesn't explain how you became a crazy cat lady."

"What part of the report have you reached?" she said.

I pointed to where I was. Lydia looked at the tablet for a moment and said, "What you should know is that when I found out they only wanted to use me as recruiting tool for adolescent bros who happened to be computer geniuses, I was ready to quit on the spot. But then I decided to pretend to go along with them. You see, I was once in the military, but I was thrown out for insubordination. I have a bit of a problem with authority. I know that's weird for someone to pursue a military career with such an attitude, but once I found myself in a position where I had to subjugate myself to men who were less smart and less capable than I was, it turned out to be more than I could bear. It's how a would-be career army officer like me ended up working as a waitress."

"You're a disgraced soldier?" I said. "That is so cool."

"Yeah, well, I thought working as a waitress at this particular restaurant would be my way back into some sort of active service. I mean, their wait-staff help wanted listings were in Soldier of Fortune magazine and mercenary sites on the dark web. And I was thrilled when I thought I had made it back into a kind of military commando service, and I didn't want to throw it all away a second time. But I wasn't just going to keep working as a real life action figure to attract nerds into the fold. My plan was to keep my eyes open and look for an opportunity to go on a real mission, and then they'd have to make me a real secret agent. I was going to try and change the system from within."

Then she paused and added, "What an incredibly stupid idea."

She turned her attention back her dumplings and I resumed reading:

REPORT FROM DAVID ST DAVID (CONT.):

After the incident of Agent Lydia Rollins's first "mission" had been put behind us, any second thoughts about bringing her into the organization were wiped away by the realization that Evan Overman, one of the computer geniuses who signed up after seeing her demonstration, was proving to be a valuable asset.

He could have worked at any big tech company of his choosing, but he told us that all of the women at these places were, as he put it, "stuck up." He told us his goal in life was to have a satisfying, intimate relationship with a woman without ever having to turn his eyes away from a computer screen. His desire to balance his personal and professional life with as limited a connection to reality as possible was something we all respected.

He told us about experiments he had been conducting on his own, and we listened with great interest. It seemed right up our alley.

For years, we had been unsuccessfully trying to break through the barriers of time and space and enter into an alternate parallel universe. We didn't know much about alternate parallel universes, but we assumed that the laws and regulations that plague our world would not apply to a parallel world, and this made it very appealing to us.

But Evan's independent forays into parallel alternative universe research did not involve humans.

It involved cats.

"I've met a lot of women who are really into cats," he told us. "They love them, I mean, they really love them, a lot more than they love me if you can believe that."

We believed that, although we didn't tell him.

"I decided that maybe getting into the heads of cats could be a way to figure out how to get into the heads of women. I've read a few scholarly works on the complexities of male/female relationships, books like 'How To Score With Chicks' and 'Get Out Of Your Way And Into Her Pants,' but I've never met a single dude who is as successful with women as any cat. I mean, cats usually move in with women right at the start of the relationship. It was my supposition that unlocking the keys to the consciousness of cats was the key to unlocking the heart of a woman."

It was becoming increasingly clear that this was a deeply disturbed and seriously unhinged young man, which made our hiring of him all the more of a coup.

He continued:

"There was this one girl that I really liked and I wanted to gain her trust, so I broke into her apartment when she wasn't there. Her cat was sitting on the floor and staring at me. I hacked into the WiFi signal in the room, but let me be clear, I was stealing her identity respectfully. I only meant to use whatever info I found against her if she didn't go out with me. I am a good person, after all."

He certainly was. Our kind of good person. He continued:

"You see, for a while I've been looking into ways of taking the concept of WiFi to the next step: going beyond the accumulation of data in the ether and the air around us and going inside the minds of people and hacking their subconscious."

I have to say, this idea got me so excited I almost ejaculated in my pants right then and there. But having already defiled a pair of trousers with a number two, I observed the better part of valor and controlled my enthusiasm.

"I'm still not yet at the point where I can extract and download human consciousness," Evan said. "But I believe I am on the verge of achieving this with cats."

Well, that was a tiny bit disappointing, so I was glad I didn't spooge for nothing. Spyware that can enter into brains and harness the dreams of humans is still the Holy Grail of any self respecting espionage agency. But achieving this with cats was a good first step; after all, animal experimentation is quite common in the field of research and development. Animal cruelty is often the first step towards a more humane world. So I was still interested enough in Evan's theories to maintain my erection.

He told us more:

"The things that cats see when they're staring off into space are unseen by the human eye. But I am now almost at the point where I can not only extract the daydreams of cats so that we can study them, soon we can enter that cat dream world and see what they see and then look out from within their

day dreams and spy on humans inside their homes from within the minds eye of a cat."

I couldn't contain my excitement any longer. I jizzed like crazy, and I think any intelligence official who loved his country would have done so as well.

We did not want Agent Lydia Rollins to know about this project. Ever since her first "commando mission," she had displayed a worrisome restlessness. She showed no interest in the new assignments we had given her, like walking amid the cubicles where our male recruits were working, smiling at them, laughing at their jokes and asking them to explain to her things she knew already, and then automatically agreeing with whatever they said. This was potentially a great morale booster and thus a patriotic contribution on her part. But she had open disdain for these tasks, and instead spent most of her time snooping around and in general not being the affable chill get-along girl her country required her to be.

I will now direct you to a different, separate report that will illuminate our dealings with Agent Lydia Rollins from the perspective of Evan Overman.

VII

REPORT FROM EVAN OVERMAN:

When Agent St David said he wanted me to write out this report, my first thought was, what is this, the year 2003? Come on, man, nobody blogs anymore. But then he explained the concept of writing as a form of communication between someone you interact with in real life as opposed to writing meant to be posted on the internet for people you've never met, and I thought, wow, sounds dumb, but okay I'll give it a try, what the hell.

I had already kick-started what was becoming the agency's biggest initiative ever, Operation Cat Scan. (Dumb name, I didn't come up with it, my suggestion, "Operation Evan Overman Is A Goddamned Genius" was rejected as too wordy.)

I was sitting at my cubicle one day when all of a sudden I looked up and saw Agent Lydia Rollins, the commando I had seen in action when I was being recruited for this job. I recognized her from that incident, and also from her many appearances in my spank bank since then.

Agent Rollins was hovering at my desk. I found this exciting at first, even more so when when she grabbed me by the collar and pulled me up to my feet towards her, knocking several Diet Coke cans over and almost toppling my computer to the floor. I had fantasized a scenario similar to this many times, but the actual reality of it was different from the role play I had devised in my mind, and I thought it was disrespectful of her to not run this by me beforehand and interact with me in exactly the way I had imagined.

"I saw several cats being brought into the building and I can't help but conclude that there is animal testing going on somewhere in the agency," she said.

"Oh, so you're a cat lover?" I said.

"I like cats, but I'm allergic," she replied. "I don't like the idea of being part of an organization that will bring harm to cats. I want you to find out where the experiments are talking place."

Needless to say, I not only knew about the animal testing, it was my idea to start doing it in the first place. But she didn't know that. My first instinct was to tell her this; after all, my advanced intelligence is one of my most attractive qualities, it's why women can't keep their hands to themselves once I've paid them to have sex with me.

"Animal testing! That's outrageous!" I said, using my best indoor umbrage voice. "I will deploy my computing and hacking skills to get to the bottom of this right now!"

She let go of my collar and I sat back down at my computer and started typing. I really felt Agent Rollins and I had a connection, so my plan was to pretend to feign interest in her concerns and then send her on a wild goose chase.

"Cool," she said. "You're putting your computer genius to good use. I'm into it."

Well, not that I'm easily swayed by a compliment, but I liked that she was acknowledging my greatness. I find that an attractive quality in a woman, not that I'm insecure or anything like that, but it's hard for my individuality to fully bloom unless I'm being given constant validation by others.

So I made an impulsive decision at that moment to give her the correct information about the location of the experiments, while still keeping it from her that I was involved in the operation. For one thing, a wild goose chase would just piss her off; she'd figure it out eventually, and then she'd be hesitant to give me another compliment. What can I tell you, her positive affirmation gave me a warm feeling in my heart. It was truly wonderful to finally meet a woman who didn't know the real, true me.

"The experiments are happening in room 4502," I said.

"Thanks, you've been so helpful," she said, and then she rushed away, around a corner and out of sight.

"Hey, would you like to have a drink sometime?" I said, but she was out of earshot when I said it, and thus didn't respond. Bitch.

But I was still basking in the glow of her undivided attention from a few seconds ago. I should point out that my willingness to give up classified information so willingly just because a pretty girl smiled at me might seem disturbing to the higher ups in this company. There is no doubt in my mind that in different circumstances, under, say, the threat of torture, I would divulge any and all state secrets that any foreign adversary would want to extract *from me. I am freely admitting that I would not stand up under any kind of interrogation, so I've already taken the liberty of sending all the classified secrets I know to every enemy we have in the world. I hope this solves the problem for everyone.*

VIII

That was it for Evan Overman's report. Here is the resumption of Agent St. David's report:

AGENT DAVID ST DAVID'S REPORT (CONTINUED):

If you've read the report Evan Overman submitted, you already know that he informed Agent Rollins about the location of the room where the cat experiments were taking place. (You also found out that for all his genius, he's a bit of a nimrod, and a cowardly weasel. As worrisome as these details might be, his complete lack of character is something we feel will ultimately be an asset to us.)

We were ready for Agent Rollins' arrival in the room where the experiments were taking place, because Overman sent us a text. The first part of the message was a request that he be reimbursed for pizza he had ordered, but he added that Agent Rollins was on her way to the laboratory with the intent of investigating and possibly sabotaging our endeavor. We were grateful for this warning, although not enough to pay for his pizza. We're made of patriotism, not money.

We had used the software he developed for us to experiment on cats, and were on the verge of a major breakthrough. The attempt to extract their daydreams from their minds seemed to be giving psychic powers to some of the cats.

The idea of psychic cats was exciting to us only if it could also lead to giving psychic powers to humans, which would be a major development in our noble quest to invade people's privacy.

We had been firing wireless electrodes (based on the coding provided to us by Evan Overman) into the cat's brains, and we wondered what would happen if those electrodes entered a human brain. Would it give them psychic powers, or, better yet, break their minds and destroy them? We were curious and had started to consider finding homeless vagrants to test this on, but now that Agent Rollins was on her way to our laboratory, we realized we now had an opportunity to conduct this experiment on someone we already knew, which gave us the appealing option of destroying a person's mind without having to make them sign a terms of use agreement.

We viewed Agent Rollins on security cameras, and as we watched her walking through the building and as we became aware of her approach, we had a quick brainstorming session. When you're coming up with ideas that can potentially turn a human into a drooling vegetable, you have to be loose and spontaneous, with a willingness to improv. This is the kind of free-flowing creativity that can really bring a spark to a group of collaborators.

But then we realized that between the twelve of us we weren't capable of generating a single idea, so we decided to just pelt her with as many electrodes as we could and see what happens.

And that's exactly what we did.

The entire lab looked like a huge electrical utility closet with rendering machines, power generators and banks of floor to ceiling computers with old-fashioned circular wheels of reel-to-reel tapes (these didn't have a practical use, but they had a stylish and cool retro look).

Amidst all this technology was the incongruous sight of four cats lounging on the hard metal floor.

Agent Rollins entered the lab. I pushed a button and unleashed a wave of electrodes that blasted into the cat's brains and then into her brain. The electrodes shot out from portals placed above the bank of computers and immediately the room looked like it was engulfed in an indoor lightning storm. We were behind a protected barrier, but Agent Rollins had no such protection and as the cosmic currents engulfed the cats and in turn engulfed her, it sure did seem like we were frying her brain in exactly the way we hoped.

Then she sneezed.

It was a monumental allergic sneeze that resonated like feedback going through a PA system, except with phlegm splattering all over the place. It was disgusting, but even worse, it abruptly turned the experiment off.

Even weirder, all four cats approached her. They rubbed up against her legs and generally acted in an affectionate way that was uncharacteristic of them and certainly had no place in a military institution.

Agent Rollins appeared shaken. Her exposure to the electronic beams had clearly impacted her mind, as we had hoped. The next logical step would have been to strap her down and remove her brain for continued study, but we were all mad that her apparent cat allergy had somehow neutralized the wave of electrodes, so we had another quick brainstorming session among ourselves and once again nobody had a single idea about what to do, so it was decided the expedient thing was to kill the cats and kill her, then get a good night's sleep and start fresh in the morning.

Unfortunately, the mind meld that had impacted her brain also put the cats on some kind of alert, like they were entering into a new advanced stage of evolution which was certainly the last thing anybody wanted.

So as our private militia entered the space to do away with her and the cats, she and the cats joined forces to fight all of them off. These soldiers were highly trained independent contractors covertly hired for their beyond-the-law reputation. So the idea that one woman and four cats could be any kind of match for them was not something anyone expected.

But as she twirled around and somersaulted and acrobatically fought off her adversaries, it was a shame there were no horny computer geniuses around to see this and be recruited into our service.

And the cats were her allies every step of the way:

An intense glance from one of the cats made some of the soldiers drop to their knees and start questioning the very nature of their existence, which needless to say was a highly unprofessional, unmilitary thing to do.

A penetrating stare from another cat managed to lock several soldiers into a staring contest, resulting in telekinetically flying objects, and making laptop computers and electronic control boards effective weapons, damaging the soldiers and worse, some expensive equipment.

Another cat scratched a wall, that's all it did, but the fallout of this simple action was several more soldiers behaving as if demons were engulfing and attacking them. These demons could not be seen or heard, which made it impossible to determine if they had entered the building without proper ID.

The remaining cat just sat and stared indifferently at everything, which in some ways made him the most annoying kitty of all.

Within minutes, all of Agent Rollins's attackers had been rendered helpless. The cats had indeed been transformed by the cat experiments. We were really onto something, it just would have been helpful if any of us had any idea what the hell it was.

By the time the fracas was over, all of our mercenaries were unconscious on the floor, and by then I had wrapped up my contribution to the melee, which was to hide and cower under a desk in a purely supervisory capacity.

When I finally emerged, Agent Rollins and the cats were gone.

We have tried to restart the experiments, but we discovered that Agent Rollins and those particular four cats are the key to advancing this experiment, but we have so far been unable to locate her or the cats.

However, we have not let this discourage us, and like other great minds who face adversity, we have bravely and boldly stepped forward and thrown more money at the problem.

"I was so messed up in my head when I left that building," Lydia said once she saw I had finished reading the report. "Getting in the middle of that experiment had scrambled my brain. My allergic reaction to the cats was the only thing that saved me and stopped the experiment, and it also caused a psychic connection with these four cats. They had been locked in that room with people who only meant to do them harm. When I arrived, they sensed that I was sympathetic to them, even though I was allergic to them. But the electrodes killed my allergies all with one gigantic sneeze. The cats knew I was their ticket out of there, but I soon realized that in fact they were my ticket out."

"We hightailed it away from the building and walked the streets of New York without incident," she said. "I continued to carry two cats while the other two cats clung to my shoulders."

"That is so sweet," I said.

"Well, their claws dug into my skin, and they weren't particularly affectionate, but helping me escape was all the affection I needed from them. And since I also helped them escape, they gave the ultimate validation a cat can give to a human: they tolerated me, and they've tolerated me ever since."

I looked over at the cats. They didn't look back. I don't think I was at the tolerated stage with them yet.

"The next day, using forged papers and fake ID, I moved into this apartment. I didn't need to wait for approval on the lease because one of the cats stared at the broker and scrambled his mind. When he came out of it moments later, I was able to convince him I had signed the lease months ago and all he had to do was give me the keys."

"Every renter in New York is going to want a cat like that," I said.

"I had considered running far away to another state or another country, but traveling with the cats seemed a bad idea, so I stayed right here in New York City. I sent an email to Evan Overman with an insincere thank you for helping me, because I did need a little more help from him, and sure enough, he was so appreciative of my kind words that he showed me how to hack into the agency's bank account and transfer the salary I would have made over the last several years into my account and covering my tracks while I did it."

"Wait a minute," I said. "Is this guy your enemy or your friend?"

"He's clearly an enemy. He's done some awful things, but he's obsessed with me. He thinks of me only as a fantasy figure, which is messed up, but it's also why he was willing to help me while at the same time helping others as they tried to harm me."

"Does not sound like the makings of a healthy relationship," I said.

"I've had worse," she said, exhaustion heavy in her voice.

I didn't pry, because I didn't want to know anything about her love life except everything.

"I was suffering from PTSD," she said. "My exposure to the experiment had jumbled my brain to the point where I didn't want to see or talk to anyone. So just staying in this apartment for a little while seemed like a smart idea. A little while turned into five years."

"Did you keep in contact with Overman?" I asked.

"No, I ghosted him pretty quick, and ironically, the skills he gave me in covering my digital tracks prevented him from finding me until just recently, which is why I'm suddenly getting visits from paid assassins, because the agency needs me and the cats to complete their experiments. That's why I had no choice but to visit him today."

"Weren't you worried going to his place would put you in danger?"

"Yes, but he's a strange, demented dude. In a weird, sick, twisted way, everything he does, he does to impress me."

"That is sick and twisted," I said, wishing like hell I could come up with some elaborate way to impress her.

Suddenly, her television started blinking on and off.

"That's him," she said. "He told me he was going to contact me later today. He said he had something to show me that would make me fall in love with him. That ain't happening, but I'm hoping he'll give away secrets that will help me fight back against the agency."

She went to grab the remote, but then turned to me and said, "You'd better stay out of the view of the TV. He'll be able to see into the apartment, and it's better he not know that you're here."

Why, because he'd be jealous? I liked that idea. I stood to the side of the couch and watched as Lydia turned on the TV.

The same view of his sad apartment that I had seen earlier came on the screen. Evan Overman was standing close to the camera, speaking directly into it.

"Hello, Lydia," he said. "I so enjoyed your visit today. You're not going to believe what you're about to see. I did it! After months of trial and error, I've broken down the wall between the human world and the world of cats. We are now able to get inside their subconscious and see the day dream world that cats see. This is a major breakthrough in science, and a milestone in world history, which I know would normally be above your head because you're a chick, but I think you're going to dig it because it involves cats."

Lydia looked like she wished she could punch her fist through the TV screen and pulverize his face. "You're talking a bunch of nonsense," she said. "Why don't you knock it off and…"

She said no more, because at that moment, the television screen became filled with a white light, and then that white light engulfed Lydia's entire apartment.

We were both immediately transported to another dimension, the alternate world deep inside the collective subconscious of all cats.

Yeah, the afternoon was starting to get weird.

One moment we were standing in her apartment, and then the next thing we knew Lydia and I found ourselves engulfed in a kind of grey nothingness. We seemed to hover in midair for a bit, then we plunged downwards. It occurred to me that this would be a cool ride at a theme park, and then I remembered that I hate theme parks, and then I remembered that I've never been to a theme park, and then I thought to myself, would I really hate it so much if I went to a Star Wars or a Marvel-themed attraction at a Disney theme park? Was my stance against theme parks just an affectation, something I had invented about myself just to make me feel cool and superior? Then I remembered that I was probably about to die so it was a shame that it was only during my last moments of life that I was confronting my own pretentious attitude towards theme parks.

Then we landed on the ground. Neither of us was injured because we hadn't been falling so much as hovering in a downward direction. The haze around us began to clear, and then I looked up and saw what looked like a million twinkling stars.

Except they weren't stars. Once I adjusted my sight, I could see they were an endless constellation of eyes. And then looking a little longer, I saw that those eyes were attached to cats, millions of cats, all staring right at us.

"Oh my God," Lydia said. "There's no one looking after my cats. I wish I knew which pair of eyes belonged to them so I could make sure they're okay."

"I hope you won't think that allowing myself to be sucked into a parallel vortex is a bad reflection on my cat-sitting skills," I said.

"Never mind that," she said. "Whatever this is, you can be sure the people behind it have nothing but bad intentions. We've got to find a way out of here and get to the laboratory in the agency where this whole thing was hatched. We have to shut it down!"

So we ventured forward, or at least what we guessed was forward. Underneath the starry night sky of cat eyes, there was a vast endless vista before us, a surrealistic desert dotted with objects and figures I couldn't quite make out. It was undeniably cool, but there was a dark sense of impending doom. I hadn't thought of it much before, but I don't like it when there's an impending sense of doom.

In the distance, I could see some birds flying towards us. Birds do fly, so nothing unusual about that, right? But as they came closer, I could see that these winged creatures had human heads and human faces. They all wore the face of actor Tom Selleck, whom I recognized both from TV, and from Lydia's enhanced premium cable lineup. His most famous show, Magnum PI, was a bit before my time, but I like stuff that was before my time. However, it really wasn't my cup of TV. Selleck's main fascination to me was the historical fact of him being the original choice to play Indiana Jones in Raiders of the Lost Ark, but being unable to do so because of his commitment to the aforementioned TV series. I once wrote in an online forum that of course I was glad Harrison Ford played the part, but I didn't think Selleck would have ruined the movie if he had played the lead. Well, you'd have thought I had made some sort of blasphemous pronouncement, considering the backlash I got.

The Selleck face we were seeing on all the birds was not the dashing Indiana Jones-could-have-been of his youth, It was a lived-in, weathered face, covered with the scaffolding of age. But regardless, it was a face on heads attached to dozens of flying birds, and that was what we had to contend with.

And the birds were talking all at once, so I couldn't make out what they were saying, but Lydia figured it out pretty quickly.

"They're all trying to sell us reverse mortgages," she said.

"But why?"

It was a reasonable question. I was not a homeowner and even if I were, I was not of an age where that type of thing would be a consideration.

"Cats watch a lot of television," Lydia explained. "And a lot of cats tend to live with the kind of people that watch the kinds of TV shows that feature reverse home mortgage ads. So when you combine the interest that cats have in birds with the kind of TV they watch, the result is a manifestation of that in their hidden daydream world."

"That's a good theory," I said. "But I have a different one. As you might know from watching your super double secret premium cable lineup, Tom

Selleck has a top secret gig as a host for the top secret briefings Pentagon officials give to the President. So maybe he's tied into this whole experiment somehow."

She thought about this for a moment, and didn't seem to agree, but this was not the time or the place for a stupid argument about anthropomorphic TV spokespeople, not that there ever is a time or place for that.

The birds, or should I say, the winged reverse mortgage spokesmen, swirled around us. It felt menacing, but on the other hand they weren't swooping down to attack us or anything like that, which was a relief because as birds and as reverse mortgage spokesmen, they were double predators.

But the din of their collective sales pitch was overwhelming. It was hurting our ears. If this continued for a few more moments I might go deaf, which, granted, might not be so bad considering I'd never have to listen to another reverse mortgage pitch again, but still, I liked listening to music and THX and Dolby surround sound, so I wanted to keep my hearing.

I thought maybe if l could somehow communicate to them that I had been not unkind to Tom Selleck in an online Indiana Jones forum, they might be willing to leave us alone, but on the other hand I thought they might be so thankful they'd engulf us and literally kill me with kindness. And it could all turn hostile once they realized I've never seen High Road To China, Selleck's unsuccessful attempt to star in an Indiana Jones movie without being Indiana Jones.

It then occurred to me that I had accumulated way too much information about the dashed movie star dreams of Tom Selleck. It wasn't doing me any good. Knowledge isn't always power, you know.

So we did the only thing we could do: we ran. The birds continued to hover above us. What Lydia now said surprised me: "Do you have any identification on you?"

Well, I wasn't old enough to drink, but, like the dedicated geek I was, I did have a library card. I took it out as she took out her drivers license. "Hold up your card and show it to the birds," she said.

We both did so. We held the cards over our heads and waved them at the flying beasts. They hovered and looked at us for a few moments, giving our identification cards a close look, then they flew away.

"They saw our identification and realized we're both too young to be in the reverse mortgage target demographic, so they left us alone," Lydia said.

"Well, that explains it," I said. "I don't know what it explains, but I guess it explains something, even though what you just said makes absolutely no sense whatsoever."

"Welcome to the universe of cat daydreams, I guess," she said.

We walked deeper into the catscape. I wasn't sure if my presence in this strange new world would change or influence me in any way, but it did cross my mind that a reverse mortgage seemed like a sensible proposition, so the process of my brain being broken had already begun.

XI

Next we came across an area where several stages were set up.

"Seems like we're in some sort of theater district," Lydia said.

"Theater district?"

"That's what it looks like. Maybe while they're sitting around apartments, cats in our world watch plays performed in an alternate reality."

"So when cats are sitting on couches and staring off into space, they're really watching plays?" I asked.

"The ones who like theater, I guess," she said. "It makes sense. A lot of cats are drama queens, right?"

"What you are saying right now is totally insane," I said. "But what disturbs me is that it's not even the most insane thing I've heard today."

"I don't think it's crazy," she said. "My cats aren't the only ones in my apartment who stare off into space. I do a lot of it myself. I look into the abyss and see plays and movies, most of which depict scenes from my own life. Moments of bad decisions that repeat over and over again. If ever there was a theatrical experience that I should walk out of, it's these shows. But the more I watch, the more paralyzed on my couch I become. It's a high definition streaming service fueled by regret."

"Cool," I said. Then, realizing the inappropriateness of what I said, I added, "sorry, I was just trying to hold up my end of the conversation."

Mercifully, she ignored me and we walked through the "theater district." We passed a stage that had a bed where two cats were sitting. But when I looked closer, I saw that, like the birds we had just encountered, the cats had human heads. I recognized them, but I wasn't sure from where. Then I saw the billboard over the stage and I had my answer; the sign read: "Tonight only: Robert Wagner and Stephanie Powers in 'Same Time Next Year.'"

Another stage was bare except for two other cats, also with somewhat familiar human heads, lounging side by side. The sign above them read, "David Soul and Paul Michael Glazer in 'Waiting For Godot'".

And another, bigger stage had a bunch of cats with human heads wandering all over the place. These faces I immediately recognized, but when

I saw the marquee for their play, I was a bit taken aback: "The Brady Bunch in 'The Color Purple.'"

Lydia and I both flinched. "Yikes," she said. "What an incredibly miscast play."

"There's a whole seventies TV vibe going on here that's very odd," I said. "With imagery from Hart To Hart, Starsky and Hutch, The Brady Bunch, not to mention Tom Selleck. I don't understand it."

And speaking of Tom Selleck, which I've been doing a lot lately, way more than I ever thought I would in my lifetime, the reverse mortgage birds returned from the sky and swooped down towards the stages. They were louder and fiercer than ever.

"What's happening?" I asked, as if logical explanations were an actual thing around here.

"I honestly don't know," Lydia said.

I thought about it for a moment and said, "Wait, I have a theory. I think it's possible our presence in the theater district has inflamed the birds."

"How so?"

"The bird/human hybrids think we're an audience for the plays, which makes them feel threatened by the cat/human hybrids, who they now perceive as potentially successful actors, which brings out their resentments because as reverse mortgage spokesmen, they feel like showbiz has-beens, totally washed up in the theatrical profession."

"I agree with you," Lydia said.

"Really?" I said. I was excited that I might be starting to impress her.

"Yes, I agree that it's a theory. A crazy, half-baked, divorced-from-reality theory, but a theory nonetheless."

"Our divorce from reality was finalized the minute we entered this realm," I said. "But I think I know what you're thinking: it's a crazy theory because none of these cats were in TV shows that lasted as long as Magnum P.I. None of them even came close to being Indiana Jones, so why would the Tom Selleck/Reverse Mortgage birds have any jealousy towards them?"

"A good point," she said, then added, "…would be helpful right now. That wasn't it."

The birds were now swooping down and threatening the casts of the plays.

The David Soul and Paul Michael Glazer cats were fearfully swatting at the birds, evoking the timid characters from Waiting For Godot more than the badasses from Starsky and Hutch. The Robert Wagner and Stephanie Powers cats were trying to hide under their stage bed in an awkward flailing way that diminished their natural panache and charm. And the Brady Bunch cats just continued to culturally appropriate a text they had no business going near in the first place, which frankly made me root for the birds.

But regardless, Lydia motioned for me to grab a folding chair and we we both jumped up onto a stage and swung the chairs at the birds. We didn't hit them, we were just trying to get them to go away. Neither of us wanted to hurt them because they were animals after all, even if they were animals who had been surprisingly funny in the Kevin Kline movie, "In and Out." But they were animals. Sort of? I guess?

Much to our relief they flew away.

"I didn't realize it, but going on stage was the best thing we could have done," Lydia said. "Now the plays are playing to an empty audience again, so they're not threatened anymore."

"So you do agree with my theory?" I said, the neediness in my voice louder than the birds.

"Yes, I never should have doubted you. And to make sure the birds stay away, we'd better do a scene from the play so the birds think we're actors in the play, not audience members," she said. "Let's pretend we're actors in Same Time Next Year."

"My knowledge of things from the nineteen seventies only goes so far," I said. "I know that the real title of Same Time Next Year is not Same Time Next Year, Episode Four: A New Hope, but beyond that, not much."

It's true. The Alan Alda/Ellen Burstyn movie version had been on basic cable one time and but I watched Transformers: Dark of the Moon instead. (It was bad, but my dissection of it in a Reddit thread was incendiary!)

"Same Time Next Year is called that because it's about a couple that meets to have sex once a year," Lydia said. "That's pretty simple, so I think we can improv it. You start."

"Uh, okay," I said, my voice going up several octaves. "Um... Let's meet and have sex once a year."

"Okay, deal," she replied. "We'll meet and have sex once a year."

She shook my hand as if we had just made a corporate business arrangement. Then she looked up at the sky. What looked back were the twinkling eyes of a million cats.

"The birds are gone," she said. "We can move on. Let's get out of the theater district. Good job."

Well, if that was my debut in show business, it was an unpromising start, and I'd like nothing better than to say that my stiff, awkward, impersonal handshake with a beautiful older woman was a formative coming-of-age experience for me, but I'm afraid that's not the case.

XII

We moved on from the theater district and then we came across what looked like a giant building made from cushions. Underneath it, there was a tunnel. On top, a sign read, "Couch Pavilion." It looked like a particularly comfortable convention center.

Lydia stopped and looked at the structure.

"I guess the only way forward is to go through the tunnel," she said. "But I don't know, there's something here that doesn't seem right."

"Compared to what happened before, why does this suddenly seem weird?" I said.

"I don't know, things are starting to seem...a little on the nose, maybe? This whole alternate universe is coming off more like something a human would come up with, not cats."

"But cats love couches," I said. "A couch pavilion in a cat world seems obvious."

"That's exactly the word: obvious," she said. "Maybe too obvious. But regardless, we have no choice but to enter the tunnel."

Once inside the tunnel, it looked like the space was filled with amusement park bumper cars that were whizzing all over the place. But a closer look revealed they were not bumper cars, they were human-sized bottle caps.

"Okay, this makes sense," she said. "I'm sure that every cat in the world dreams about the bottle caps they slap underneath couches. What we're looking at may very well be the secret garden of bottle cap cat dreams."

It almost sounded lyrical the way she put it. But as the bottle caps zoomed towards us it was immediately apparent that if any one of them hit us we'd become seriously injured.

The caps were all from Coca-Cola company products. I knew this because there were Coca-Cola banners hanging everywhere. The fact that this alternate cat universe appeared to have product placement definitely gave credence to Lydia's idea that something was not quite right.

She grabbed my hand and we ran through the tunnel. I followed her lead as we swerved and dodged each deadly bottle cap that came towards us.

The caps sped by in a blur, but I thought I might have seen one or two with promotional offers inside the caps that could be redeemed for cash prizes. I couldn't help but think that there was a sense of commerce infusing this whole thing, which is not something you expect to find in a nonlinear surrealistic landscape.

We emerged on the other side of the couch pavilion without being the victims of a twist-top hit and run, although we came close a few times. We were exhausted. We gave ourselves a moment to catch our breath.

"Cats are so lucky they don't really know what happens to the bottle caps once they slide under the couch," Lydia said. "They assume it's something exciting like what we just went through. But it's really just an inert object sitting in darkness. Life is like that, isn't it? The reality of things compared to our imaginative fantasy is always so disappointing."

"I bet you're fun at parties," I said.

She laughed. "This is the closest I've been to a party in years," she said.

"Same here."

Were we bonding? Were we finding common ground based on our mutual talent for being depressed? It seemed like we might be on the verge of getting to know each other, but then, at that moment:

"Pretty impressive that you survived the couch pavilion," a voice said. I looked around and saw a guy standing behind us. He was just a few years older than me. He had a bad haircut, but I couldn't hold that against him. He was a bit stocky, but not fat; you got the impression he struggled with his weight, and I certainly wasn't going to hold that against him, either. But his outfit...well, it was like armor made from electronic parts - a keyboard on his chest, twinkling modem lights all up and down his arm, pants that seemed made from hard drives. It was nerdy as all get out, but being a nerd myself, I knew I shouldn't hold that against him, either.

But something inside me made me hold all of it against him. All of it.

"I thought I might see you here, Evan," Lydia said.

It was Evan Overman. I had seen him on his premium cable channel, but he looked different in person. I didn't know him but I was already judging him so at least I was on the right track.

He then gave me the once over. "Who's the geek? He's not supposed to be here."

"Geek?" I said. "Sorry, but I don't consider that an insult. And if you're going to do cosplay, try and come up with something that doesn't look like it was purchased at a Tron-themed thrift store."

"I am wearing the most advanced computer-based wardrobe in the world," he said. "It's the latest fashion, except I'm the only one brilliant enough to wear and operate it."

"The only one dorky enough is what you mean," I said.

Pow! I really zinged him, didn't I?

"If you don't watch yourself," he said, "you'll find out why they call me Eradicator One."

"You're Ejaculator One?" I said.

"It's Eradicator One!"

"Oh my God!" I said. "I know you from the internet. I've had flame wars with you. I'm the guy who named you Ejaculator One on Reddit. I've gotten in huge arguments with you about The Last Jedi, Zack Snyder, Gamer Gate..."

"That was about ethics in gamer journalism!" he yelled.

"Okay, enough of this," Lydia said, like a mom breaking up a fight between her children, which was definitely not the vibe I was going for.

"What the hell is going on?" she asked Evan.

"Well, the bigwigs at the agency opposed me, but I insisted that you be transported here," he said. "I wanted you to see my impressive achievement before we resume our experiments with you. For the limited time you have left being alive, I hope you'll be my girlfriend."

"I'm not in the habit of going out with people who are complicit in animal experimentation," Lydia said.

"I have nothing to do with that."

"This whole operation is your brainchild!"

"Yes, true, but I'm conflicted about it," he said. "I'm a very complex person, you know. There's a duality within me. On the one hand, I'm capable of monstrous behavior. But on the other hand, I'm also capable of pretending I'm not capable of monstrous behavior. So you see, I am deep! How can you not find that compelling?"

"Very easily," Lydia replied, her voice expressing deep douchebag fatigue.

"Look," he said. "I could be a wonderful person if you just approved of everything I did, and showered me with constant affection. But you won't, so this is all on you."

Lydia opened her mouth to say something, but then the sound of motor vehicles filled the air. We turned and saw a bunch of food trucks driving towards us.

"Food trucks," I said, pointing at them. "This must be the food truck district."

They looked exactly like the food trucks I saw on the streets of New York City, except these were selling cat food — wet fancy feast type of stuff and dry kibbles, all in containers hanging on the side of the trucks.

"Why would there be food trucks in a cat dreamscape?" Lydia said. "Cats live indoors. Sure, they see food, and they see trucks driving by the windows. But food trucks? Almost never."

She turned to Evan. "What's going on?"

"Look," he said. "The mind of cats are unfathomable. Just because we have entered the world of their daydreams doesn't mean we can understand everything about them. The process of unlocking their minds is just beginning. All I know is, when you're dealing with killer food trucks, what you end up with is culinary carnage."

The phrase "culinary carnage" sounded familiar to me. I knew I had heard that expression before but I couldn't quite remember where. Then I looked at Evan's stupid face and it suddenly dawned on me.

"Wait a minute," I said. "That phrase, 'When dealing with killer food trucks, what you end up with is culinary carnage' was written in block letters in a Reddit thread posted a while back by... Ejaculator 1."

"Eradicator 1!"

"You did a whole rant about how Hollywood was so lame because they wouldn't buy your screenplay called... Killer Food Trucks!"

"It would have been a killer movie, and 'Culinary Carnage' was a killer catch phrase!"

"So how is it that this so called alternate reality that we're walking through feels like a novelization of your screenplay?" I asked.

"What's going on here, Evan," Lydia said. "Fess up."

"Okay, okay," he said. "This cat dreamscape is inauthentic, but only in the sense that it's completely man-made and built by the agency. State of the art special effects were created and financed through a secret fund."

"But why?" Lydia said.

"Well, um, you see, my original theory that the dreamscapes of cats could be entered by humans and used to spy on people turned out to be not quite workable," Evan said. "The agency spent several months and billions of dollars pursuing research into making my theory a reality. Finally, after one failure after another, I had to tell them, 'sorry, my dudes, I come up with a lot of my theories while wasted on edibles, I don't think the spying on humans through the subconscious of cats thing is gonna work out, hope you're not mad.' But as pissed as he was, Agent St David decided to build a cat dreamscape anyway, so he redirected the agency's resources into creating a fully populated surrealistic dreamscape which would trick the higher ups in Washington into allocating more money to the agency. That's what you're looking at now."

"So this so- called alternate universe is just a scam to get more funds for the agency?"

"Well, come on, there's more to it than that," Evan said. "We're skimming off the top! I'm finally getting the kind of money I would have gotten if I had worked at Silicon Valley, before you fooled me into working here."

"I fooled you? I had nothing to do with that scam."

"Look, I'm not some adolescent, like this jerk tagging along with you here," Evan said. "I'm a grown man. An adult! So I'm mature enough to know that everything bad that happens in my life is always a girl's fault."

Lydia got madder, but I was confused about something.

"Wait a minute," I said. "It really did seem like we were transported from the apartment into an alternate universe."

"I sent a signal through the TV that knocked you both out," he explained. "I happen to be at the forefront of new technology advanced weaponry that will soon enable cable companies to injure cable viewers in their homes. It's a way to crackdown on people sharing their passwords with friends and family. Anyway, soldiers were sent to Lydia's apartment. You were removed and placed in the artificial vortex portal I helped develop. It really seemed like you were instantly transported here, didn't it?"

He then pointed at me and said, "They weren't supposed to bring you along, but mistakes are made in the fog of war."

It honestly did seem like we had been instantly transported to an alternative universe. I wasn't going to say it out loud, but it was a cool special effect.

"Take a good look," Evan said, gesturing at all that was around us. "You can't deny the awesomeness of my vision, although we spent so much on special effects, like the sky-scape of cat eyes, that we had a limited budget for using the likenesses of celebrities. Corporate sponsorship from Coca-Cola helped, but due to a lack of funds, instead of dealing with overpriced modern stars, we had to settle for licensing the images of actors from the 1970s like Tom Selleck, Stephanie Powers, and Robert Wagner, although let me tell you, RJ is a class act all the way."

I could barely contain my jealousy that he got to meet the guy from Austin Powers, and there was more:

"I also had the opportunity to meet some awesome Hollywood special effects people. They were really interesting. It sucked that we had to kill them when they were done."

"You what?" Lydia said.

"Hey, don't worry! They'll be featured in the Oscar's 'In Memoriam' montage."

Lydia was livid. "This is all so pointless and stupid," she said.

"Hey, don't forget, I tried being nice to you and I got nowhere. So I thought if I came off more like an evil bad boy, you would find it attractive. You forced me to take a different tact."

"I forced you?" she said, seething. "Your behavior is my fault because I wouldn't behave a certain way you wanted me to, is that it?"

"I can't help myself. I love you." he said.

"You love me, but you're willing to kill me?"

"And you're uncomfortable with that?" he asked. "Man, you do have a fear of intimacy, don't you?"

Lydia ignored this and asked, "Where exactly are we?"

"We are right underneath the agency in midtown, where, by the way, experiments are about to be conducted on your four cats."

"What?!!!"

"They were also knocked out by the signal I sent through the TV and they were also removed from your apartment. Their psychic abilities were an unexpected outgrowth of the agency's experiments. Those cats are the reason the agency has been trying to find you all these years."

Lydia became agitated. She was as distraught as I'd ever seen her. "We've got to get up there, right now and stop them" she said.

"You'll only go where I say you'll go," Evan said. "In this world, I'm the God. I'm the God! I control everything."

He punched some keys on his computer keyboard vest. The food trucks increased their speed and barreled towards us.

Lydia also punched the keys on his computer keyboard chest, but by that I mean she punched him hard in his chest with her fist, knocking him to the floor, damaging the keyboard, and rendering him unconscious.

She then grabbed me and pulled me out of the path of the oncoming trucks, which were unmanned and computer operated. They just missed hitting us and then careened into the walls of the couch pavilion. The entire building might as well have been made of soft cushiony airbags, so it was weird that the trucks exploded and bust into flames anyway.

"Come on," Lydia said. "We've got to get up the laboratory and save my cats!"

"But how would we find our way out of here? How will we…"

She pointed off in the distance. I didn't see what she was pointing at at first, but we stepped over Evan Overman's limp body and I followed her and then as we ran towards it, I saw what she saw: amid all the surrealistic fantastical Hollywood-made soundstage imagery, there was a door with an "Exit" sign. She opened it, revealing an ordinary looking stairwell.

It just goes to show that if you look beyond the incredible beautiful visual splendor around you, you can always find the mundane in the world, as long as you open your mind to it.

XIII

When we got into the stairwell, Lydia said, "You know what, you were never supposed to come along for this. The first thing I should do is help you get out of this building so you can go home and be out of danger, but I'm so worried about my cats…"

"I'll go with you to the laboratory," I said. "You might need my help. As far as I'm concerned, my one hundred dollar cat sitting fee covers all of this."

She smiled. "You're funny," she said. "You have no business being as socially awkward as you are."

I was touched. It would have been the perfect moment to say something in response, but I didn't because, you know, I'm socially awkward.

We rushed up a couple flight of stairs. She opened a door which led to a hallway with a bank of elevators. "We need a pass to get on the elevator," she said. "I used to have one but I don't anymore, which means we'll have to run up the stairs the rest of the way."

"What floor is the laboratory on?"

"The forty-fifth floor," she said.

I live on the second floor of my apartment building, and I almost always take the elevator, so this was bad news. But then she said, "Wait, someone's coming."

We stepped back into the stairwell and she peered through a crack in the door. A regular plain looking man in a business suit, who gave off the impression that his dream as a child was to be a bureaucrat when he grew up, walked down the hallway. Lydia grabbed him from behind, knocked him out, and dragged him back into the stairwell. She searched his pockets and found his magnetic security pass.

"Thank you, Craig Johnson, assistant director of Accounts Receivable," she said, looking at the identification on his badge. "You've been a big help."

We got into an elevator. Lydia swiped his card and we were on our way to the forty-fifth floor. We arrived there and walked towards a door at the end of the corridor. Lydia knew exactly where she was going.

"This is the laboratory," she said. She swiped the card in the digital pin pad but it didn't work. "You need special clearance to enter this room," Lydia said. "Something the assistant manager of accounts receivable doesn't have. Oh well."

And so she kicked down the door. It was a thick door and it took her three kicks to do so, but that door was ultimately no match for her.

The one drawback of it taking her three kicks was that it gave enough time for those inside the room to prepare a greeting for us. Agent David St David, the man who had recruited Lydia in the first place, along with a flank of armed guards, all pointing machine guns, were waiting for us as we entered the room.

"Agent Lydia Rollins," Agent St. David said. "Welcome. Long time no see. "We've been expecting you. Have you come for your cats?"

He tilted his head towards a glass partition on the right side of the room. All four of her cats were in there, looking as irritated as you'd expect cats who had been uprooted from their home to look, and also as irritated as you'd expect cats to look under any circumstance.

"The partition prevents them from psychic communication with you, or with any of us. However, that will all change as we resume our experiments."

"What experiments?"

"The ones we are going to conduct with you and the cats. After all of our experimentation, your psychic bond with them is the most significant thing that happened. When you and the cats left us, we had to build that fake alternate cat universe to keep the illusion of progress until we found you and the cats again. And now we have."

"You're going to kill me?"

"No, absolutely not. We're going to keep you here as a prisoner and continue to study your brain and its bond with the brains of the cats. Sure, within the process, you will become a vegetable, but we'll make sure you don't drool all over the equipment."

He then gave me a hard look and said, "I don't know who your friend is, but him we can get rid of right now."

I had never been so frightened in all my life. Even that time I posted a picture on Instagram of my Avengers screen saver on my computer, and then panicked when I thought the photo also included a dropdown menu of my browsing history. It was a false alarm, but for a moment I was so scared. This was worse.

The guards aimed their weapons straight at me. But suddenly the entire room was engulfed in smoke.

Oh, wait, I left out an important detail: the reason it was engulfed in smoke was because I had pulled a smoke bomb out of my pocket, threw it on the floor, and it exploded. It was the little item I had taken from one of the paramilitary visitors who had invaded Lydia's apartment.

Right now the dudes with machine guns couldn't see us, so they couldn't shoot us. It was the first time in this whole adventure that I had been the proactive man of action. It didn't feel as good as I thought it would. The fact that in all likelihood I was going to die anyway somehow diminished the sense of accomplishment I should have had.

I could hear chaos all around us, but no shots were fired. What I did hear were punches and kicks being thrown and people falling to the floor. As the smoke cleared, I saw that Lydia was holding a machine gun and all of the soldiers were lying on the floor.

"Open up the partition!" she said to one of the defeated guards. Apparently dying in the service of his job was above his pay grade because he immediately went to a wall, pushed a button, and the translucent barrier that separated the cats from everyone else slid open. But then some kind of magnetic vacuum effect sucked Lydia's weapon and all the weapons in the room up to the ceiling.

"The upper brass fought me on having that feature put in, but obviously it was worth it," Agent St. John said. He was standing on the left side of the room behind a control panel, which had build-in machine gun barrels that were sticking out of the front.

"Guess I'm going to have to kill both of you, and the cats. Then we'll have to start from scratch. Another setback for our project and It's your fault."

"It's always a girl's fault, isn't it?" Lydia muttered.

A feeling came over me, a feeling that had become quite familiar: the feeling I was about to die. I will never get used to that feeling if I live to be a hundred.

Agent St David started to pull a lever that acted as a trigger and I braced myself for a moment of severe pain followed by an afterlife of eternal damnation (all this constant danger had turned me into a pessimist). I heard the terrifying sound of machine gun fire, but the splatter of bullet holes and blood did not happen to my body or Lydia's body, but to Agent St David's body. He fell dead to the floor, which I could only see as a positive development.

I wondered what had happened, and then I turned and saw that Evan Overman had entered the room. He was holding a smoking machine gun and had a smug, self-satisfied look on his face that suddenly made me lose the will to live.

He had just saved our lives and I could tell he was going to be really conceited about it, and that seemed like it might be too high a price to pay for not dying.

"And here I am, just in time to save the day," he said. "Exactly like Han Solo."

"In Star Wars?" I said.

"It's called Episode Four: A New Hope, idiot," he snapped.

"The analogy is weak," I said. "First of all, Han Solo was a lovable rogue, never a bad guy, whereas you are all bad guy."

"You're welcome," Evan said. "Thanks for being so appreciative that I just saved your life."

"And I do appreciate it, even though it means I have to be alive to hear you get everything wrong about the Star Wars mythos," I said.

"I know from your online posts that you have no idea what is and isn't Star Wars canon," he retorted. "Have you even read the graphic novels or novelizations? You don't know jack about..."

Lydia intervened. "I want to thank you sincerely for saving our lives," she said to Evan. "It was really sweet of you."

She smiled and his face showed an expression of rapture that was stupid, ridiculous, and made me so jealous.

But then she added: "However, you're the one who put us in danger in the first place, maybe just so you could be the hero, I don't know, I'm not going to waste any time trying to figure out your twisted logic and diseased mind. What I do know is that you are a criminal, and you're going to pay for your crimes."

Evan faced this harsh truth like a man: he turned around and ran away.

For a moment it looked like Lydia was going to chase him, but then she turned and looked at her cats and remembered her priorities.

"Let's grab the cats and get out of here," she said. "You take Edna and Jerry, and I'll take Duke and Hayley."

Lydia grabbed two of them, the other two didn't look like they wanted to be taken, especially by me, but Lydia gave them an intense look and I picked them up without incident. There was an understanding between Lydia and the cats that for now at least they should ignore their natural instinct to scratch the hell out of me.

I regretted that I had ever thought of anyone else as a crazy cat lady, because I was running down a hallway in a midtown office building with two cats under my arms. I was as crazy a cat lady as anyone who had ever crazy cat lady'd.

We got into an elevator. Before the doors closed, we saw a man, rubbing his head and staggering unsteadily, walking down the hall.

Lydia threw a security pass at him.

"Thanks for helping us, Craig Johnson," she said. "And keep up the good work in Accounts Receivable."

He looked at us blankly, having no idea who we were, but he picked his pass up off the floor and I bet he was glad to have it back.

The elevator doors closed and we were on our way down.

"Maybe we shouldn't get off at the lobby," I said. "I bet they'll be more guards waiting for us."

"I'm sure you're right," Lydia said. "But I can tell by the look on Jerry's face that he's preparing us for this."

I tilted my head slightly and saw that Jerry, the gray haired cat that I was holding — painfully, I might add — was staring downwards in a state of deep concentration. It was as if he had pushed the "L" for "Lobby" button in his own mind, and was psychically getting there before we did.

The elevator doors slid open, and my prediction was right, there were at least a dozen armed guards awaiting our arrival. But they were all on the floor, sobbing uncontrollably. They didn't look like they could use their weapons if they tried. This was a relief to me, but I couldn't help but also wonder why it is that when a person has his thoughts psychically manipulated to the point where he takes a cold hard look at himself and becomes lost in introspection, it inevitably results in tears and terror. Is there ever a circumstance where taking a good look at oneself results in light hearted happiness? I guess not.

This cat's ability to force men to be brutally honest with themselves is one of the most lethal, debilitating superpowers ever.

We headed into the lobby, but the mayhem wasn't over yet. Edna the cat suddenly leaped over to the security desk and tore into the lobby guard's microwave burrito, hissing and pawing at the air in a way that made the guy at the desk run away screaming.

This had nothing to do with our situation, the poor man who worked at the check-in desk wasn't trying to prevent our escape at all, the cat was just being a dick.

Lydia handed me Hayley, so she could grab Edna. I think she felt that picking up Edna mid-burrito was probably too dangerous a task for me, and she was undoubtedly right.

Carrying two cats each, we ran out into the street and saw that Evan Overman was already handcuffed, in custody. Two policemen were leading him to a squad car.

"Congratulations!" I said to one of the cops. "You've captured a dangerous criminal."

"Really?" the cop said. "We're just arresting him for being a public nuisance. He was standing in the middle of the street, dressed in this ridiculous computer outfit, blocking traffic and yelling 'I'm the God, 'I'm the God!'"

"Was he messing around with his computer keyboard as he did this?" Lydia asked the cops.

"Yes, he was," one of the cops said.

"I thought so," Lydia said. She gestured towards Times Square, which was a few blocks away. We could see that on every digital billboard in the area, big and small, the worlds, LOVE ME were printed out in big block letters. It was even written on all the digital "walk/don't walk" traffic crosswalk signs.

It was so sad. Sadder still was that for all his insanity he had used his considerable computer skills to hack the city's electrical grid expressing a sentiment that gave him a commonality with just about everyone else in the world. I tried not to think about this.

"I'll be providing the proper authorities with much more information that will put Evan Overman away for a long time," Lydia said.

This caused Evan to turn to Lydia and say, "I'm going to jail, aren't I?"

"In all likelihood," she replied.

I expected Evan to fall apart but he actually had a look of New Hope on his face.

"Ladies love prisoners, don't they?" he said.

"What?"

"Charles Manson had a girlfriend. It's true. Maybe this'll be the thing that finally makes me a chick magnet."

He now looked happy and optimistic.

Lydia could only wince. "The ability of certain men to always live in a fantasy world no matter what will never cease to amaze me," she said.

She was addressing this to Evan, and to me, and to all men. But I knew I wasn't like Evan at all. I mean, he lived in the kind of fantasy world where there is no recognition of how great The Last Jedi is, and the Snyder cut of Justice League is treated like a masterpiece and not the bloated mess it is. Unlike Evan, I've got street smarts and have accumulated enough life experiences to properly evaluate the movies and TV shows I spent all day and all night watching. Obviously, despite being a few years younger than him, I have achieved a much higher level of maturity.

Lydia and I, and the cats, took an Uber home. Lydia and I didn't say much. We were overwhelmed by the events of the day, and also, $98 for a trip from midtown to the Upper East Side had left us speechless.

Our silence continued as we reached the hallway between our apartments.

"Well, it's been fun," Lydia said.

"In a crazy, dangerous way," I added

She smiled at me, then put the key in her lock. She opened the door and the cats all rushed inside, but we lingered for a moment.

"I'll see you around," she said. Then she gave me a warm, friendly, but not particularly sensual kiss on my cheek, although it was certainly sensual by my standards.

Before she entered her apartment, Lydia turned and said, "We did some good. We may not have saved the world, exactly, but we certainly saved my cats. You know, I've grown to really love my cats over the past few years. I've become so devoted to them."

"Really, I hadn't noticed, crazy cat lady."

"Okay, wiseass," she said, smiling. "The point I want to make is that as much as we might love house cats, we don't want to be like them. They are content in their limited world of four walls, but the more our human lifestyles resemble their lifestyles, the less of a life we have. My shut-in days are over. I'm going to get out of the apartment more."

"Will you want me to take care of the cats while you're gone?" I said. "I am available," I said. "I'm available a lot."

"Don't be!" she said, forcefully. "I'm going to get out more and you should, too. For God's sake, go live a real life, not one based on fantasy TV shows and sci-fi movies. Get out of your own head and into the real world."

She had a good point, and I was determined to take her advice.

But then I remembered that a new Mandalorian episode was dropping and I didn't want to miss it before the internet became filled with spoilers. I frantically unlocked my door. I couldn't get back into my apartment quickly enough.

But then I thought, wait, what am I doing? As the protagonist of this story, I should be experiencing some sort of personal transformation. As I've pointed out in many online missives, a good character arc is essential to a hero's journey. So I resolved to take Lydia's words to heart. She was right: I need to come out of my shell and experience the world outside my apartment and find out what life is really about.

So I went back to my front door and peered through the peephole.

THE TRUE CRIME PODCASTER IN APARTMENT 3C!

PROLOGUE
"DEATHOVERTURE"

I might be a little too old to be starting a podcast, and a little too young to be living in my building. It's on the Upper East Side of Manhattan, and a lot of the residents here are even further along in years than I am. They may even have one foot in the grave, which now that I think of it could be a good title for my podcast, because it's in the popular true crime genre, and its main focus will be a popular topic…murder!

I'm not as old as some of my neighbors, but believe me, I'm old enough. I was born in the late 1950s and I lived a long time in the pre-internet/cable/mobile phone/computer age. The world has changed considerably during my lifetime and for many years I didn't notice those changes, which I hate to admit because when I was young my ambition was to be a detective, and the ability to notice things comes in handy in that line of work.

At one point I did have another ambition: to be a musician. Specifically, a prog musician. In case you don't know, notable examples of prog are Emerson, Lake and Palmer, King Crimson, Yes, Moody Blues, Gentle Giant, Pink Floyd (early), Hatfield and the North, Henry Cow, and Genesis, before Peter Gabriel left the band and they sold out by making music that people liked.

Prog is the most difficult form of music to play. It's a little bit of rock 'n roll and a lot of complicated, intricate, poly-rhythmic composing and playing, with offbeat time-signatures and many, many, many notes. It requires vast technique and years of study and practice. It's the kind of music Beethoven would have played if he had put a little more elbow grease into his work.

This was a problem for an aspiring prog musician like me, because back in those days, the 1970s, the heyday of prog, I spent most of my time smoking pot, drinking beer, listening to records, and watching TV. It's hard to develop virtuoso music skills when you're usually too baked to even pick up an instrument, much less play one

I would love to have been a dazzling guitarist or keyboard player or drummer, but in the prog jungle, if you don't spend any time learning how to play an instrument, the system is stacked against you.

So becoming a detective — my other great passion in life — seemed much more doable, because all my pot smoking didn't go to waste: I watched a lot of 1970s detective TV shows while I was high: Mannix, Barnaby Jones, Cannon, Columbo, Rockford Files, Baretta, Hawaii Five-O, you name it. As far as I could tell, to learn how to become a detective, you had to watch a lot of TV, and in this case I really put in the work.

I was what some might call an armchair detective, which was cool with me because I've always enjoyed sitting down.

Of course, it is a bit of a paradox that as a dedicated pot head I was constantly breaking the law, but I was never too wasted to lose my basic interest in crime solving. And most of the TV detectives I liked were not strictly law enforcement officers. They were private investigators who played by their own rules, and like me, they were always butting heads with the police, except in their case it was because they were poking around in areas where they weren't welcome, and in my case it was because I was urinating on public property.

Being a detective seemed like a much more doable goal than being a prog musician. Based on what I could see from the TV shows I watched, all you had to do to be a private investigator was open an office, hire a secretary, and then just hang out until people came to you for help with a missing persons case or a kidnapping or a cover up of a murder or some such thing. Seemed like a pretty easy gig, as long as you solved the case before the final freeze frame and executive producer credit.

Of course, these are TV shows I'm talking about, but if you're listening to a "true crime" podcast, you are interested in real life, right? Well, I assure you, all the times I spent getting wasted and watching TV did in fact happen in real life, but the reason I'm dipping my toe into these podcasting waters is because I was personally involved in a notorious real-life case you've all heard about, so it's the perfect subject for my first-ever True Crime podcast.

ACT ONE
"DAYS OF MURDER PASSED"

Did you know that Brandon Penny, the keyboardist and arguably the main creative force behind the classic 1970s prog band Galactica Anathema, was murdered? You always thought his death was a tragic accident, didn't you? Well, I know the truth, and that's what you're going to find out about here, exclusively, for the first time.

Brandon Penny was a prog rock star who never did anything in a small way. He never wrote a three minute tune when a thirty minute "suite" would do. His compositions weren't songs, they were filibusters, and me and my high school friends were huge fans. We purchased every Galactica Anathema album and went to all of their concerts whenever they traveled from England to America. Our devotion to their cosmic brand of complex harmonically challenging music was such that we stayed with the band till the very end, when they released their final magnum opus, the double album, "The Seven Sinus Infections of Kahlil Gibran."

That record has many detractors, but me and my best friends Becky and Jim loved the whole double record, all three songs.

When it was announced that Galactica Anathema was coming to the Nassau Coliseum, we rushed to get tickets. We lived not far from there in Garden City, Long Island. Turns out we didn't need to rush, we easily got great seats. We didn't realize the popularity of the band was waning. The public's taste was changing I guess, but at least we were open-minded enough to continue thinking the same way about their music as we always had.

I would love to tell you that Becky was my girlfriend but I'm afraid that wasn't the case. She had short brown hair and big brown eyes and a face like a foreign film actress, but without the subtitles. People thought there was something going on between us because we were together a lot, but the truth is that this was a period in Becky's life when she was experimenting with lesbianism. Later she went to college, then moved to New York City and started a family with a long time girlfriend and had two kids, eventually marrying when the laws finally allowed it. So I guess you can say the experiment was a success.

But she was my good friend, as was Jim, a total jazz-head who only tolerated a few non-Jazz musicians, Frank Zappa being one, Galactica Anathema being another. Jim never shaved and at this point was barely growing facial hair, so the lower half of his face was like a torn carpet next to the pimply linoleum that was the upper half of his face. His hair was stringy and unwashed, which was the fashion of the time, although Jim would have denied that he ever adhered to any fashion.

Jim hated anything that smacked of commercialism. He considered all bands that indulged in melody or rhythm to be total sell-outs. I was more open to different groups and artists, but I think Jim and I bonded because back then he had even less friends than I did. I don't know if his musical tastes these days are as subversive and revolutionary as they used to be because now he's a wealthy hedge fund manager and prominent GOP donor who doesn't return my phone calls.

But that night all those years ago when we were just three teenagers going to see Galactica Anathema at the Nassau Coliseum, Becky, Jim and I were psyched and ready to worship our prog gods.

The section of the auditorium where we sat near the stage was packed, but the crappy seats in the back and up in the rafters were mostly empty. If the ability to get people to pay for lousy seats is the ultimate sign of a band's success, the career of Galactica Anathema was in double album-sized trouble.

"I read in Rolling Stone that their new album is not selling well," Becky said.

"Which confirms to me that their latest album is the best one yet," Jim said. "The buzz I'm picking up is that they're becoming hated. I really respect them for that."

The lights dimmed and the crowd cheered. But then when the announcer said, "Ladies and gentlemen, please welcome to the stage, Red Herring," you could feel an audible groan of disappointment throughout the hall. Damn, we were going to have to sit through an opening act! I didn't recall seeing Red Herring listed on the bill, and this was an egregious oversight on the part of the promoter. A lot of people who attended these concerts tried to time their drug use for exactly the moment when the band they came to see hits the stage. Arranging it so that you are peaking on acid precisely when your favorite trippy song is playing is important to many prog consumers, so it was irresponsible for those in charge not to take this into account.

And Red Herring couldn't have been more mismatched with Galactica Anathema. They were a punk rock band, and their look was like if the Ramones went trick or treating on Halloween dressed as the Ramones. They played the kind of minimal punk stuff that was just becoming popular, but not with prog fans! Their songs were loud and fast, usually based around one or two cords. And you couldn't understand what they were saying, which is another thing that made it so different from prog. With Galactica Anathema, you could understand every single word, without ever really knowing what the hell they were talking about. That's the sign of true artistry.

The only ones enjoying them were a bunch of groupies dancing in the aisle. That's how lame their music was: you could dance to it!

At least their set was not too long. They were booed as they left the stage by everyone except the groupies, who cheered wildly and then headed for the stage door. They were all dressed in ripped clothes with safety pins and leather jackets, the look that was becoming big with punkers back then. I mean, these groupies hadn't even come to see Galactica Anathema, they were there for Red Herring! The band and their groupies were very much in the vanguard of what was happening in music then, and everything they did smacked of cultural relevance. How sad is that?

But twenty minutes later, the sadness went away as the lights dimmed and Galactica Anathema finally hit the stage.

Brandon Penny was his usual regal self. Dressed in a black cape, he looked like a Phantom of the Opera who forgot to have his face disfigured. Not that it was easy to see his face — his flowing blonde hair, like a Lady Godiva with virtuoso keyboard skills, covered half his eyes and went down almost to his torso.

But when he smiled, you could see his teeth, or should I say his dentures.

Like a lot of British people, his teeth were not his best attribute, but rather than cover it up, he made no secret of his having purchased custom-made dentures that were designed to look like piano keys. To be honest, it was kind of gross. The teeth made to look like black keys gave the impression that he had been eating his own feces. But by the standards of United Kingdom oral hygiene he looked fine.

The bass player and singer, Bryan Seaford, was throbbing away on his axe and moving about the stage like a restless leprechaun, and his flowing Lord of the Rings beard only added to this image. His mad skills on the bass didn't prevent him from being a showman.

He was almost as well known as a health food nut as he was a musician. He had recently made a public service announcement promoting vegetarian eating with Linda McCartney. But I have to say he seemed a little slower than usual and it looked like he had put on some weight, although he was trying to hide it with a flowing wizard's robe that seems even more appropriate on a prog musician than it would on a wizard.

Noel Carson, the drummer, was obscured behind a row of tom-toms, huge cymbals and *triple* bass drums. He was banging on the skins at his usual rapid pace. He had amazing technique, the result of a lifetime of intense discipline, but many people assumed that because he played so fast and frenetically, and because he had the skeletal look of a sun-deprived zombie, he must be an amphetamine addict. He was offended by this misconception and he made a point of telling interviewers that he wasn't an amphetamine addict, he was a *prescription* amphetamine addict

The band was playing one of their big numbers, the title track from their classic concept album, "Loch Ness Monster, Ruler of Atlantis." I had seen them perform this composition before, and the stage effect had been a big movie screen with wavy water going back and forth. It was effective and quite evocative of what it's like to be in an underwater city. In fact, it usually made half the audience seasick and lots of people puked. That's how good it was.

But this time they went for a different visual motif. As Brandon Penny played a flank of electronic keyboards, seemingly all at once, a huge barrel of water was dumped all over him from above the stage.

This led to a truly spectacular stage effect. As he became drenched in the water, electric sparks shot up all around him, from his hands to the keyboards and all over his body. He shook and gyrated and his face turned pale. It was very cool, but he screamed out in pain, abruptly stopped playing, and fell to the floor. It was very dramatic, but I think the music suffered even more than he did.

I mean, the song still had another forty five minutes to go, so this was jarring and unexpected. Even less expected was that he had just been electrocuted to death, which for all his extraordinary musical ability was still going to make performing the rest of their set a bit difficult.

The audience grew restless, and started clapping in unison to get the music to continue.

At a loss, Bryan Seaford announced, "Is there an electrician in the house?" But that caused feedback and a bit of a spark so he and the drummer quickly ran off the stage.

The show was ending early, which meant everybody was going to beat the traffic, and that was no comfort to anyone.

But as Galactica Anathema's set was abruptly ending, my work was just beginning.

This concert was now a crime scene, and it seemed a sure bet that I was the only person in the auditorium who had watched enough Quinn Martin productions to handle this case.

The opening act had been Red Herring. The main attraction had been Galactica Anathema. But now the encore was murder.

ACT TWO
"TALES FROM TOPOGRAPHIC MURDER"

"Let's go backstage," Becky said.

It wasn't a crazy proposition. Becky was friends with Lisa, who worked for the Nassau Coliseum. She told Becky she could arrange backstage passes for us and we'd be on the guest list.

I didn't know Lisa. She was a bit older than Becky and didn't go to our school. Earlier, when I had asked Becky where she knew Lisa from, she said, matter-of-factly, "she's my lover."

My instincts as a detective told me this might mean they'd had sex with each other.

As the rest of the audience reluctantly exited the auditorium, collectively grumbling that they wanted their money back, Jim, Becky and I headed toward the backstage entrance.

"What a great concert!" Jim said. "I think dying in the middle of the first song was an edgy, envelope-pushing move. I respect Brandon Penny for having the integrity to not finish a song that might be compromised by his being alive to play it. It makes me even more interested in what he's going to do next."

We arrived at the backstage door. The look of disappointment on the bouncer's face when he saw we were on the backstage list was deep and profound. I think this scarred him even more than the scars that already dotted his unfinished construction site of a face. You could tell that turning people away was a big part of who he was, and giving a trio of average looking nobodies All-Access passes and letting them enter an exclusive sanctum was a moment where he wondered if his life had meaning anymore.

We were lucky we arrived backstage before the police got there. The press wasn't there either; nobody in the world of rock journalism gave a damn about prog bands anymore, and the word hadn't yet filtered to the mainstream media that someone they never heard of had died.

So at this point, I, with my extensive experience of watching Mannix and Barnaby Jones, was the closest thing to a crime-solver there. I was an independent investigator who played by his own rules, but the badge I was wearing said only, "GUEST."

Backstage, there was a palpable feeling of shock and disbelief in the air. Becky's friend Lisa came over and they embraced. Back then, LGBT people were much more circumspect when it came to public displays of affection, so Becky and Lisa were taking a risk because many people were offended by the sight of two people of the same gender exhibiting kindness and compassion towards each other.

Lisa had a kind of all-American look to her, blonde and bright, like a Brady Bunch sibling who was too cool for potato sack races. She wore a grey jumpsuit with a "Nassau Coliseum" logo on it that wasn't exactly feminine, but all backstage Coliseum employees wore this, so her secret was safe, even though I'm not sure she considered it a secret.

Lisa had not watched the show. Her job entailed a million tasks, including making sure the dressing room was stocked with the healthy foods that Bryan Seaford, the band's bassist and singer, insisted on. It was in the band's contract rider; their lawyers had neglected to include more practical conditions like "musicians must not be electrocuted to death during the concert."

There were roadies and stage crew members milling about in various states of distress and confusion.

And there were groupies. Well, one groupie. I had earlier seen her dancing to Red Herring. She had a dyed red mohawk, tight leather pants and a ripped t-shirt covered with silkscreen drawings of safety pins, something so meta it almost made my head explode.

She was in mourning. But not for Brandon Penny. She was grieving for the ride on the band bus to Manhattan she had missed.

"I was supposed to go into the city with Red Herring!" she complained to one of the roadies. "The other girls went with them to The Mudd Club, but I missed out because I was stupid enough to go look and see what happened when I heard that big electrical noise go off. I ran over to look at Brandon Perry lying on the stage, as if I cared. By the time I got back they had all left without me. This sucks!"

She tried to go back onto the stage, but the Roadie blocked her path.

"Where do you think you're going?" he said.

"I've decided to have sex with Brandon Penny."

"But he's dead!"

"I know!" she replied. "So if I do him now, it will make me notorious. I'll be the first band girl to have sex with a dead rock star. It's the only way I can get any respect for doing it with a prog musician."

"You are so vile!" the Roadie said. "Either leave now, or have sex with me."

She turned away from him. She was pissed, but I'm not sure sex with the Roadie was completely out of the question.

I was surprised a groupie would have such disdain for prog. For one thing, if the sexual technique of prog band members is anything like their musical technique, they can probably keep going for a long time. And I bet the positions they assume are in interesting time signatures.

The Groupie tried to walk away, but the Roadie quickly grabbed her.

"You know" he said. "Brandon Penny's famous keyboard dentures are missing from his mouth. Some ghoul grabbed them right after he died. Was it you?"

"No, I saw one of the Nassau Coliseum crew take them," she replied. "He ran away with them just as I came over to the body."

"Which crew member? What did he look like?"

"I don't know. He was a small dude, wearing a 'Galactica Anathema' baseball cap that covered half of his face. I only saw him from behind."

Well, whoever that person was, his behavior sure was suspicious, as was the groupie's behavior. She had been closer to the crime scene than almost anyone else, so that made her a suspect in my book. I wanted to interrogate her myself, but at that moment, Peter Payne, Galactica Anathema's manager, burst into the room.

I recognized him from an article I had read in Melody Maker magazine. For a behind-the-scenes guy, he was pretty famous. He was fat and sweaty, with prematurely curly grey hair that was as wild and unruly as he was. Known for his volcanic outbursts and underhanded business dealings, he had been sued by some of the biggest names in rock, and at this point Galactica Anathema was the only band he still managed.

Although his criminal personality made him an automatic suspect in my mind, he had no motivation I could think of for murdering the lead musician in his only popular band.

"Everyone get the bloody hell out of here!" he screamed. "There's been a horrible tragedy. What's wrong with you people?"

"He's right, you know," Jim said to me. "The world has lost one of its most uncompromising musicians and this is a time for mourning and reflection and… are those free beers?"

Jim had spotted a huge cooler full of iced Heinekens on a table up against the wall. Lisa whispered to us, "I think everyone is going to be kicked out of here pretty soon, but I know of a remote storeroom nearby where you guys can hang out and not be bothered."

So we grabbed as many free beers as we could and Lisa led us to a hallway and then to a a freight elevator which took us to a restricted room on the other side of the arena, a few floors up. We were right behind the crappiest seats in the Coliseum, but we had a room all to ourselves where I could sit back, drink some brews, smoke some more weed and chill out while I continued my active investigation.

Lisa was still on the clock, so she left us there and said she'd come get us in a little while. The storeroom was filled with toilet paper and cleaning supplies. It was not the most appropriate setting for three people who had been in search of cosmic musical prog transcendence, but there were boxes to sit on and an adjoining bathroom, which was convenient considering all the beers we were drinking.

Jim, reflective as always, especially when puffing on a doobie he had just been passed, said, "Do you realize we witnessed history tonight? It's like we were there at the Kennedy assassination, except this was even worse because JFK was killed before he had the chance to make a solo album."

"But this wasn't an assassination," Becky said. "It was a mishap, an accident."

"I wouldn't be so sure of that," I said. "It might be an accident. Or it might be…" I stood up for dramatic effect, "…murder!"

I got up so quickly, blood rushed to my head, and that combined with all the pot and beer made me dizzy and I almost passed out. I quickly sat back down. (The thought occurred to me that this was also different from the Kennedy assassination in that blood was rushing into a brain instead of spouting out of one, but I would have rather not have had that thought.)

I wasn't about to let the fact that I was so stoned I could barely move impact my murder investigation. I would just have to continue digging deeper and peeling back layers of intrigue without going anywhere or doing anything.

And my time wouldn't be wasted regardless of how much I was wasted. As I drifted in and out of consciousness, I asked myself an essential question:

What would Mannix do?

Mannix had been cancelled a couple years earlier, but he was rerun on Channel 9 every night, so his exploits were still a big part of my education, and I often wondered what he would do in any given situation.

In this case, get something to eat was my deduction. Not that his show had an abundance of scenes where he had a meal, but I realized right then and there that I was really hungry, so I assumed Mannix would be, too.

"Let's get something to eat," I said. "There's got to be some food around here, and not that healthy crap set out for Galactica Anathema in the dressing room."

"Maybe we can find the concession food that they sell in the arena," Jim said. "I bet it's nearby."

"Need I remind you guys that this place is probably swarming with cops by now," Becky said. "We could all get into trouble if we make a stoned pilgrimage to find munchies."

"But we're out of weed," I said. "So we're not in possession and they can't arrest us for being stoned."

"They absolutely can arrest us for being stoned," Becky said.

She was right. I was so high I had forgotten to be paranoid.

"But damn, I need something to eat," I said. "And I need to solve this case."

"What case?"

"The murder of Brandon Penny."

"Jeez, you are high, aren't you?" she said.

Becky was perceptive in that way. If she had applied her talents to detection, and also altered her basic biological desires, she and I could have become a husband and wife team of millionaire sleuths, like Hart to Hart, although I'm not sure how we would have pulled off the millionaire part.

But we were all craving snacks, so Becky, Jim and I left the storeroom and wandered the back halls of the auditorium. We saw a door that said, "Concessions." This seemed like a good bet.

I opened the door, but there were no concessions and it wasn't even a room, it was an empty concession stand that looked out into the back rows of the seats in the highest part of the stadium rafters.

We heard voices. Becky and Jim quietly rushed back through the door. But I crouched down on the floor because I was feeling dizzy again. I stayed on the floor as I peeked up to see who was speaking.

Two men sat in chairs in the very back row of the stadium. One of them I recognized as Peter Payne, the manager of Galactica Anathema. He was scary looking from any angle, so I stayed quiet.

I didn't recognize the other guy sitting with him. As big and bulky as Peter Payne was, this guy was thin and almost sickly looking. Payne was an intimidating guy to say the least, and this other dude looked like he was born intimidated.

Payne handed him a wad of cash. "Here's your payment," he said.

"Thank you for being cool about this," the other guy said. He stuffed the money into an envelope. I saw that the envelope had an "Ice Capades" logo on it. There was also a blue stain on it, like the remnants of a blueberry snow cone. It reminded me of how hungry I was.

"That stage effect I provided did not go the way it was supposed to. It went horribly wrong," the guy said.

"Never mind that," Payne said. "Just make sure you don't tell anyone you or I had anything to do with it."

"I won't. Believe me, if the people I work for in the Ice Capades knew I did business using Ice Capades resources with an outside vendor without their approval, I'd be in big trouble."

"So keep your mouth shut," Payne said. "I know the Ice Capades are loading into the Coliseum tomorrow, so don't say anything to anyone about it. And don't forget: this was an accident. An accident!"

They both got up and left. Luckily, neither one of them heard my stomach growling as I eavesdropped.

"Oh my God!" I said to Becky and Jim when I found them in the hallway. "Peter Payne had Brandon Penny murdered!"

"Why do you say that?" Becky asked.

Before I could answer, we walked around a corner and found ourselves face to face with two uniformed policemen. I had been watching a lot of Adam 12 lately, so I was a little freaked out.

"What are you doing here?" one of the cops said. "You're in a restricted area."

"We've got backstage passes, pigs!" Jim said, showing them the badges attached to our shirts. It was uncool of Jim to go out of his way to antagonize them, but the all-access passes had made him power-crazy.

Needless to say, they lined us up against the wall and padded us down, but we weren't holding. However, we did smell like a Cheech and Chong album that had had a million joints rolled on it, so I was worried they were going to bust us anyway.

Then another cop showed up, but he was plainclothes.

"Who are they?" he asked the other cops.

"Some stragglers," one of the cops replied. "They're clean, at least the outside of their bodies. There's enough contraband still inside their lungs to send them to Attica, but I'm afraid we don't have jurisdiction over that. We were about to let them go."

"I want everyone who is still in the building to remain here," the plainclothes cop said. "Take them to the auditorium and put them with everyone else."

We were taken to the seating section in front of the stage. We were right back where we started. A bunch of people were there, including Peter Payne, the chief suspect as far as I was concerned. The surviving band members, Noel Carson and Bryan Seaford, were also there. Also, Becky's friend Lisa, the Groupie, and various roadies and crew members, along with the Ice Capades guy.

"This is cool," Jim whispered to me. "We're gonna get to hang out with the bassist and drummer of Galactica Anathema."

"They look pretty distraught," Becky said.

She was right. They had haunted, grim looks on their faces. They were already in deep mourning for their lost income.

I realize that's a cynical thing to say. I guess for me, the idealism of the mid-seventies was already beginning its descent into the ennui of the mid-to-late-seventies.

The head cop on the scene, a police lieutenant, stood and faced the assembled group. His hair was plain, his face was plain, his body was plain, his whole demeanor was plain. Being a plainclothes detective suited him.

"Hello," he announced. "I'm Lieutenant Douglas of the Nassau County Police. Something terrible happened here tonight, and I want to get to the bottom of it."

"Why is someone from the bloody police here?" Peter Payne said. His thick British accent filled the huge cavernous space. He stood up for emphasis. "It was a bloody accident and I'm going to sue the goddamned venue!"

So that's it! He wanted to make a killing from his killing: a big payout from a lawsuit So I had my motivation! Damn, I was good!

I was feeling so confident about myself that I had the balls to stand up and say, "Hey, Lieutenant, if you're going to detain us, how about feeding us?"

The Lieutenant looked at me with the same disdainful look that was the standard issue police response to all hippie stoner dudes of that era.

"If I get some food in my stomach, it will help me help you with your investigation," I said.

It was not what he wanted to hear. "If you want to help me, you'll shut up and do as you're told, you stoned out hippie freak!" he said. "But since I do need you all to stay a while, I see no reason why we shouldn't feed all of you. I'm sure the band has lots of catered food they can share with everyone."

"That health food crap?" Jim said under his breath. "Damn, I'd rather go hungry."

The band's bass player, Bryan Seaman, stood up and said, "That food is for our special organic diet. It was specially designed for our particular biology. If anyone eats it besides us, it could cause diarrhea that will go on longer than one of Noel's drum solos."

"What you ragging on me for?" Noel Carson said. "Crikey, things are sad enough as it is."

"I'm sorry, mate," Seaford said. "I'm in a state of shock and not thinking about what I say. But come on, your drum solos are bloody self-indulgent."

They both got in each other's faces and stared angrily at each other for a long time. Prog musicians never do something in a minute that they can do for several minutes. It looked like this might eventually lead to a violent confrontation in the next hour or so, but then a uniformed cop the Lieutenant had sent backstage to find food came into view pushing a cart of snacks. "I went into the inner sanctum of your inner dressing room, and I found this food," he said to Seaford and Carson. "I'll tell you one thing. If this is health food, I think I'm going to become a health food nut."

It was a large tray of Twinkies, cupcakes, cookies, and a few celery sticks that were obviously only there as a spoon for the bowl of mayonnaise-based onion dip that sat right next to them.

"Oh, thank God, celery, my favorite food!" Seaman said as he broke away from his confrontation with Carson and made a big show of eating the stalk of celery. But as he chomped into the vegetable, he shoved cupcakes and cookies into his pockets. He was trying to do this discreetly, but he wasn't pulling it off.

As for me, I was openly happy that a Twinkie had just entered my life. As Seaford watched me eat, he couldn't resist: he pulled a cupcake out of his pocket, loudly removing the wrapper.

"Well, when in Rome," he said, laughing as if this was a madcap lark, a one-time cheat on his strict health-food regime.

I had already deducted that his organic food persona was a ruse that covered up deeper issues he had with what was possibly a junk food addiction. He was far from the slim, spandex-clad rock god of the band's first album cover. In other words, he was a man who kept secrets, which fascinated me as a detective, but at that moment I was more focused on the hostess snack I was shoving into my mouth, which seemed to me in my stoned munchie-addled state like a priceless treasure, a Maltese Falcon with cream filling.

Once I was fortified with enough processed sugar and flour, I was ready to continue my investigation. I went over to Seaford and said, "If you don't mind my asking, did anything seem suspicious to you tonight?"

"Oh, you mean aside from Brandon Penny getting bloody electrocuted to death?"

"Well, aside from that, did anything seem out of the ordinary?"

He stared at me for several seconds, and seemed like he was maybe about to call the police, but there was no need for that, the police were already there, Lieutenant Douglas specifically, who was standing right behind me.

"Why are you talking to this idiot?" he said to Seaford. "Anything you have to say about the events of tonight, you can address to yours truly."

"Look," Seaford said, not talking directly to Douglas, or to me, more like he was addressing a New Musical Express journalist inside his own head. "Brandon was always doing things that were unexpected. It's one of the things that made him such a great musician. He always surprised you, like tonight's stunt with the water."

"You didn't know about that?" Lieutenant Douglas said. (I was pissed, because I was about to ask him the same thing. This cop was stepping on my toes, and as an independent investigator, I was the one who was supposed to be stepping on *his* toes.)

"Hell no, I didn't know about it," Seaford said. "The idea of dropping a bunch of water on electrical equipment is the dumbest thing anyone has ever done! I feel awful that he died, but I'm more than a bit relieved that I escaped with my own life."

He suddenly started to sway a bit. "Oh, bloody hell, I need to lie down," he said.

He lay down on the floor. He was already crashing from the sugar.

Lieutenant Douglas glared at me with the exact same contemptuous look I've gotten from a million school teachers. "You stay right where you are," he said. "And stop pestering people."

He walked back over to consult with a couple of other police detectives, secure in the smug knowledge that he was all over the case. But my powers of detection caused me to notice something he had overlooked: I picked a candy wrapper up off the floor that had fallen out of Seaford's pocket when he had grabbed the cupcake from it. It was a wrapper from an already eaten Crunchie-brand candy bar, which at the time was available only in England.

Seaman suddenly got up and grabbed the candy wrapper from my hand. "Don't you dare touch that!" he said. "I'm going to keep this forever. It will remind me of Brandon. He wasn't the health food fiend that I am, you know. His favorite thing in the world was Crunchie candy bars. We both always brought one candy bar each on stage with us and ate them immediately after the show. It was a ritual with us. We had been doing it at every show since we started out playing gigs in tiny London clubs. But he never got the chance to eat one this time. After he was killed, and I was sure the stage was safe, I went back to retrieve the Crunchie bar from his dead body. But it wasn't there anymore. Someone had stolen it."

"You were going to eat it, weren't you?" I said.

"In tribute to him!" he said. Then he started crying, either for his dead friend, or for the candy bar he would never get to eat.

How did this fit in with the case? I had no idea. But I was going to keep digging until I found out, but just then, I was having my own sugar-crash. I felt the need to lie down on the floor, and I did.

Jim came over to me and said, "Hey, shouldn't you have mentioned to the cop that Peter Payne knew about that water stunt before it happened?"

"No," I said. "I don't want any of the suspects to know what I know."

"Suspects?" Jim said. "Man, you're really into this detective stuff aren't you? Things are really getting noir around here. I feel like the Miles Davis recording of Green Dolphin Street should be playing right now."

"I'm going to get the bottom of this case," I said. "And I'm not going to rest until I do."

Then I fell asleep.

ACT THREE
"BRAIN SALAD HOMICIDE"

I was poked back into consciousness by Lieutenant Douglas.

"Wake up, stoner" he said.

Ah yes, the classic conflict between private investigator and police official was unfolding before my bleary eyes.

"I need to know two things," he said, pulling me to my feet. "Who are you and what the hell do you think you're doing here?"

I told him my name, which took me a second to remember, then I said, "I came here to see the band, then me and my friends Jim and Becky stuck around because Becky's friend Lisa got us backstage passes."

"Well, stick around some more," the Lieutenant said. "I'm not done with you yet."

This was a bit disappointing. I wanted him to say something like, "Stop sticking your nose where it doesn't belong, Mannix."

As he was walking away, I said, "I hope you don't think I'm here to get in your way. I'm here to help. I'm a detective like you. Not to rub your face in it, but I've probably watched even more TV cop shows than you have."

"I don't watch TV," he said. "I never have time, and if I did, I wouldn't watch a bunch of crime dramas, which all of us real cops hate."

Wow. It was amazing to hear him admit how unprofessional he was. Just another case of cop burnout, I guessed. It was obvious that solving this case depended on me, because this guy, who apparently had never once heard an announcer intone the words, "A Quinn Martin Production," was in no condition to do his job.

"Listen you little weasel," he said. "Do you really think you can come in here and be a detective just because you came up with the idea of being one while you were high?"

Wait, how did he know that? Maybe he was better at his job than I thought.

"You're part of the generation that doesn't appreciate the hard work your parents put into working their butts off and raising you," he continued.

"You've been handed everything on a silver platter, so you think you can just sail through life. Well, you stay out of my way and stop poking your nose into places where it doesn't belong!"

Bingo! He said the exact thing I had always dreamed a police guy would say to me. It was like being given a diploma, which was cool, because getting an actual high school diploma had lately been seeming more and more unlikely.

Lieutenant Douglas walked away, completely bypassing the Ice Capades guy. Should I have told the Lieutenant what I knew about the payoff between the Ice Capades guy and Peter Payne? Yes, probably. But being the maverick I was, I played by my own rules. I was going by the private detective credo: when your partner is killed, you have to do something about it. I didn't know quite how that applied here, but it was a private detective credo I had heard somewhere, so I was sure it had something to do with me.

I went over to the Ice Capades guy, who was nervously pacing in the aisle next to the seating section where everyone was. Bringing a hippie veneer to the amusements industry, he had long black hair and wore a tie dye shirt, suspenders and bell-bottoms.

I decided to play it cool and not let him know that I knew he worked for the Ice Capades.

"So, you work for the Ice Capades, huh?" I said. "Must be cool."

"Wow," he said. "I never heard the words 'cool' and 'Ice Capades' used in the same sentence before. It's not cool. I'm just doing this job to pay the rent until I achieve my dream of working in an art form that has some cultural cache."

"What's that?"

"Dinner Theater. One time when I was tripping, I had a profound cosmic vision that I would one day work at the Burt Reynolds Dinner Theater in Jupiter, Florida on a production of Barefoot In The Park staring Wayne Rodgers and Jessica Walters."

Wait a minute! Wayne Rodgers had recently been in an episode of Barnaby Jones that I saw, and Jessica Walters had been in a Mannix. And on top of that, Burt Reynolds was Dan August, although that cop show had been cancelled years ago, so maybe the Ice Capades guy was trying to put me off the scent.

I couldn't be sure, but one thing was clear: this suspect and I were engaged in a deadly game of cat and mouse. I had to move forward carefully. A single slip up could send me careening into an intricate web of intrigue and suspense. I was on full alert, although it took me a moment to remember what we had just been talking about.

"What are you trying to cover up?" I said. I had lost the thread of our conversation, and this seemed like a dependably generic thing to say.

"What are you talking about?" he replied.

"There's something you're not telling me."

"Not telling you? For christ's sake, I just revealed my fondest, most secret wish. I've never told anyone about my cosmic Barefoot In The Park vision. I was even about to share my idea for an avant-garde production of Please Don't Eat The Daisies, an immersive theatrical experience where the audience members are encouraged to actually eat the daisies and everyone gets food poisoning and then they're all put in ambulances and the entire third act takes place in an actual Hospital Emergency Room. All I needed to make this happen was some money, which I was finally able to obtain, and…"

He clammed up. He had just revealed some possibly incriminating information about himself. He was in a vulnerable spot, which could help me in my investigation. I had to be cagey, and not let on too much about what I did and didn't know.

"Look," I said. "I didn't mean to upset you. I only meant to imply that you may possibly have been involved in a conspiracy to murder Brandon Penny. But please don't take it the wrong way."

"You stay away from me!" he yelled. "If you know what's good for you, you'll stay away!"

He was making a scene. Everyone else that was gathered in this part of the auditorium was staring at us, including Peter Payne, who started walking over towards me.

Uh oh. Now this was a certifiably scary guy. Everyone in the music business was already scared of him. He had struck terror in the hearts of journalists who had written articles he didn't like, publicists who didn't properly defer to him, record executives who didn't answer his calls quickly enough, and waiters and retail clerks who didn't serve him fast enough.

I hoped he'd be a little easier on me. All I was doing was accusing him of murder.

"Is there a problem?" he said to me and the Ice Capades guy, knowing full well there was one.

"No, none at all," I replied. "I was just complimenting this guy on the spectacular stage effect he pulled off."

"Spectacular? You mean the thing that killed the leader of the band? You LIKED that?"

"Not everything about it," I said. "I didn't like that Brandon Penny was killed, I would have preferred to hear the rest of his keyboard solo, but that's just my personal taste. Reasonable people can disagree."

I wasn't letting him know everything I knew. I was just saying random stuff off the top of my head, which may not have been a great decision.

Payne was livid and seemed ready to pummel me, but then Noel Carson, Galactica Anathema's drummer, who was seated a few rows away from us, absentmindedly twirling his drumsticks, stood up and addressed him.

"What did you mean by saying Brandon Penny is the leader of the band?" he said. "I thought we always agreed that everyone in Galactica Anathema was an equal."

"Oh, come off it," Payne said. "Now that Brandon is dead we can be truthful. He was the main attraction. You're the bloody drummer. By your very nature you're never going to be the front man."

"What about my twenty minute drum solos?" Carson said, the hurt rising in his voice. "I am the center of attention when those happen!"

"Not by a long shot, mate," Payne said. "Your drum solos are when everybody goes to take a piss. Hell, I've gotten my laundry done during your drum solos. If it weren't for your drum solos, I would never catch up on my mail."

Having watched as many TV shows as I had, I knew that every now and then it was the detective's job to smooth things over between people so there could be a poignant catharsis. So I decided to step in and make things better.

I went over to Carson and said, "You resent all the attention Brandon Penny got at your expense, right? That's a pretty solid motivation for murder. Do me a favor and hold that thought, I might be able to use it later."

"Who said anything about murder?" Carson said.

"Yeah, what are you going on about, you stupid yankee twit?" Payne added. "I don't know who the hell you are, but it's a bloody outrage that you're making wild accusations while the body of the heart and soul of our band is still warm."

"Oh, so Brandon was the heart and soul of the band, was he?" Carson said angrily. "Bullocks!"

I don't know why he was saying some random word that made no sense, but the moment was rife with tension, only to be broken by the musical sound of an organ filling the entire arena.

Well, actually, the organ may have made things more tense, because the song being played was "Tie a Yellow Ribbon," a popular chart single of the era, but I would have bet money that everyone in that particular room at that particular time intensely disliked the song. Hatred of Tony Orlando, while unjustified and unfair, was something that united a lot of people back in the 1970s.

Peter Payne shot the Ice Capades guy a harsh look that was supposed to be discreet, but I totally noticed it. "That's your Ice Capades co-worker, right?" he said, under his breath. "Tell her to knock it off!"

Payne and the Ice Capades guy were giving a master class in being suspicious. The sound of the organ, which filled the entire arena, was typical of what you'd hear at an Ice Capades show, and I got the impression that this organist, whoever it was, was somehow mixed up with Payne and the Ice Capades guy, so when the Ice Capades guy walked away, I followed him, in a discreet way, because when a detective tails someone, he has to be subtle about it.

"Stop following me," the Ice Capades guy said about ten seconds later, but then ten seconds after that he reached his destination, so it turns out my surveillance skills were as awesome as I thought they'd be.

The organ was set up in a booth attached to a PA system behind the bleachers. I spotted the organist. She was a sweet looking older woman in the Barnaby Jones age-range, somewhere between ancient and dead. She had a pleasant and upbeat disposition, which made me feel embarrassed for her.

"Please cool it!" I heard the Ice Capades guy say. "The load-in for the Ice Capades doesn't start till tomorrow. I don't know why you're still here. I thought you said you were going to…"

He turned and saw me, and immediately got quiet, but the organist lady remained as chipper as ever.

"Honestly, your generation is so negative," she said. "I guess hard work just isn't 'far-out.'"

This was a searing indictment of the youth culture of the time, but she smiled sweetly as she said it. She didn't seem to have an ounce of meanness in her, so of course I immediately put her on my potential suspect list.

She stopped playing, got up and walked away, whistling to herself. She really did seem like a nice lady. I was going to hate it if I had to bust her ass.

The Ice Capades guy stood by himself for a moment, throughly chastised. The idea of not being far-out was devastating to him, as it often was to hippies back in those days.

He was having a moment of quiet solitary reflection, so I figured this would be the perfect time to approach him.

"Is there something you want to get off your chest?" I said.

"What are you talking about?"

"Look, I know you were involved in the stage effect that resulted in Brandon Penny's death," I said. "And I know you and Peter Payne are mixed up in it together. So please come clean with me. Aside from being implicated in a manslaughter charge, and going to jail for years where you'll no doubt be beaten and abused, I promise no harm will come to you."

Before he could respond, I heard the click of a gun. I turned and saw the holder and the clicker of that gun: Peter Payne.

"Let's go to a more quiet place where we can talk, mate," he said.

Two things:

I didn't think he really wanted to "talk" to me. I believed it was a euphemism for wanting to kill me.

Secondly, when he called me "mate" he didn't mean it in a nice way, as if we were going to form a friendship. It was just a United Kingdom way of saying things. Kind of dumb, if you ask me, but nobody ever accused the British of having any kind of elegant command of the English language.

In any language, I was in trouble. Murder had been in the air all evening. Except now it was my own murder that seemed in the offing. And if I was murdered, I wouldn't be around to solve it, and worst of all, I wouldn't be around to see the next episode of Barnaby Jones, which I was really looking forward to. The truth is, when you're suddenly face to face with your own mortality, you tend to focus on the things in life that are important.

ACT FOUR
"IN THE COURT
OF THE CRIMSON KILL"

Peter Payne led me through a labyrinth of hallways behind the bleachers to a remote dressing room. There were lighted mirrors on the wall, so I was going to get a clear view of my own demise.

I have to admit I was scared. I wondered if when Mannix was confronted by a bad guy, he ever wished he was safe in his house, smoking a doob, eating ice cream, and watching Don Kirshner's Rock Concert.

There was no denying that seeing a real person with a real gun pointed directly at me was truly scary, especially with no commercial break coming up to give me a moment to think of a way out.

The time had come for me to be defiant and resourceful, just like every TV detective I had ever seen in this situation. This was a moment for strength, not fear.

"Please don't kill me, dude," I pleaded. I wracked my brain for scenes on TV shows when my detective heroes were on the verge of pissing their pants, but I couldn't come up with anything.

"Listen," Payne said. "I'm warning you to back off. I can't afford to be caught up in a scandal over whether or not I was inadvertently involved in the accidental death of Brandon Penny, however a lucky break his death is for me."

"A lucky break?" I said. "How can that possibly be?

"Oh, crap," he replied. "I shouldn't have said that out loud, but it doesn't change the fact that I had nothing to do with his death."

I was confused. "How could his dying be a good thing for you?" I said. "Galactica Anathema is your only moneymaker."

"Moneymaker? That's a laugh! This band is bleeding money. Did you see the turnout tonight? Pathetic. Prog is dead. Punk and disco are the wave of the future. Right now, the only thing that can generate income for a Prog band is a spectacular death, and that's exactly what happened here tonight. Brandon Penny's death will fuel sales, not just in albums, but in merchandise, like memorial t-shirts and commemorative cod pieces. It will make me some much needed money and buy me some time while I figure out the next musical trend I can cash in on."

"But he's dead. Your number one artist is dead."

"Yes, sometimes wonderful things can happen. It's what makes this such an exciting profession."

"God, you really are evil, aren't you?"

"Of course I'm evil! Do you think I would have survived in the music business this long if I wasn't? However, that's a whole other issue, because I did not kill Brandon Penny! But if you don't stay out of my hair, there's a good chance I will kill you. Consider yourself warned!"

He put his gun in his pocket and walked away.

Whew. What a relief. He wasn't going to kill me. I guess he instinctively realized it was too early in the episode for that to happen. He hadn't convinced me that he wasn't involved in the murder, so I might still have to confront him, and the thought of this brought me close to pissing my pants again, but thankfully there are plenty of bathrooms in sports stadiums.

When I got back to the main part of the arena, in front of the stage, the band's roadies were dismantling the set and putting away instruments. One of the roadies, a heavy guy who also managed to look like a meth addict, was putting the keyboards away. He kept looking over his shoulder as if he didn't want people to see what he was up to. He seemed like someone I should keep my eye on, if I could only keep my eyes open, that is, which was becoming increasingly difficult as the night progressed.

I was tired. Sure, I understood the urgent need to continue my investigation, but I now wanted to do it from my home. where I could smoke one last joint, drink one more six pack of beer, and catch the late night rerun of Hawaii Five-O on Channel 9.

But McGarrett and Dano would have to wait, because I knew if a person was behaving suspiciously, it was my job as a detective to check it out, and something was not quite right with this roadie.

I went to the side of the stage and saw that the roadie was walking away with a bulky electronic instrument in his arms. I wanted to know what was going on, but I also knew that I couldn't let him know I was interested in what he was up to.

"Hey, dude, what's going on, what are you up to?" I said.

He turned and glared at me.

"Back off, mate," he said. "You don't know what I'm up to, but I know what your scheme is, you want to grab this instrument I'm holding. It's Brandon Penny's mellotron. I'm giving it special protection because it's the most famous mellotron in the world."

"Well, actually, an argument could be made that the mellotron used by The Moody Blues is the most famous mellotron in the world," I said.

"Shut up!" he said, and he meant it.

Maybe I should take a moment to explain that back in the 1970s, the mellotron, a keyboard-based instrument, was an essential element to just about every prog band. At the time, many of us expected the rest of musical history to be completely mellotron-dominated. It didn't quite turn out that way, but the point is, if Brandon Penny's mellotron wasn't the world's most famous mellotron, it certainly was right up there in the top five.

The roadie became more menacing.

"If you don't back off, I'm going to smash this over your head," he said.

I took his threat seriously. This guy looked like he could be a bouncer whose job it was to kick other bouncers out of biker bars. I did not want to mess with him.

But then he said, "Okay, clearly I'm not going to smash this over your head, because Brandon Penny's mellotron is going to be a valuable artifact one day, even more so now that he's dead. I'm glad that tonight was the night I advised him to sign it, right before the show."

It's true. I could see Brandon Perry's signature in big bold letters on the keyboard, made with unusual green magic magic marker ink.

"The green ink makes his signature really cool," he said. "It was lucky that one of the blokes from the coliseum crew had the marker handy to lend me. And even luckier, then Brandon went and got himself killed."

Whoa. This guy was out-suspecting all the other suspects. He had motive and opportunity coming out of his ears.

"This mellotron will finance my retirement," he continued. "For years I watched this preening twit gad about the stage getting all the glory while I did all the work. Now, the tables have turned!"

This was a dangerous and violent dude, so I knew that whatever I said next had better calm him down.

"So, you more than likely killed Brandon Penny," I said. "That's good to know as I continue my murder investigation."

Uh oh. Now he was really angry. In that instant I learned that big dangerous men prone to violence don't like being provoked.

"I've never murdered anyone!" he said. "But there's a first time for everything."

He gently placed the mellotron on the floor and lumbered in my direction, showing none of the gentleness towards me that he showed towards the mellotron.

But then Lieutenant Douglas approached us.

"What are you two doing over here on the side of the stage?" he said. "I want you both to come with me."

The roadie bent down to pick up the mellotron, but Lieutenant Douglas said. "Leave that there. Now come with me, both of you!"

The roadie was angrier than ever at me. If I thought this murder investigation was going to enter a more laid-back folk-rock kind of vibe, I was sadly mistaken.

We went over to the seats in front of the stage. The Lieutenant had gathered everyone. Seated there were:

Pater Payne, squirming in his chair, too big for his seat, unsettled, not quite sure whose life he was going to threaten next.

The Ice Capades guy. It suddenly occurred to me that since I am a detective and obtaining information is a big part of what I do, I probably should have taken the time to learn his name. But sometimes the weight of facts in an investigation are just overwhelming.

My friend, Jim. He was bored and just wanted to go home. He wasn't a suspect; I knew he had nothing to do with it, but maybe I'd be honoring his love of the avant-garde if I considered him a suspect even though there was no possible way he could be. Maybe if there had been an Aaron Spelling Production on the air in those days called something like, "The Case Files of Philip Glass," I might have pursued this line of thought but there wasn't so I didn't.

Becky was seated with her friend, Lisa. They were holding hands, discreetly. But by the standards of those days, Becky and Lisa were being brazen. Becky really was taking the whole true-and-honest-acceptance-of-one's-own-sexuality thing and running with it. The time had come for me to acknowledge that nothing was ever going to happen between us except friendship. This was disappointing but luckily I was open-minded enough to fully accept her for who she was and come to terms with it about thirty years later.

Also seated was the drummer, Noel Carson, who was playing a rapid drum solo with his drumsticks on the chair in front of him. It was interesting to note that when you remove a virtuoso musician from the context of his own drum set, his amazing skills just seem annoying. What was a tour-de-force on stage becomes just plain aggravating when you remove the theatrical setting.

Bryon Seaman, the bass player and singer, was sitting in a chair with his head tiled back, snoring. His beard and shirt were covered with cookie and cake crumbs. It was a gruesome sight in its own way, like Weegee photographing the aftermath of a sugar-crash.

The Groupie was also there. She had the look of a person whose evening had gone horribly wrong. Missing her ride to the city with Red Herring, straight into the heart of the burgeoning punk scene in Manhattan, was a devastating blow.

For all her punk bravado, there was something lovely and endearing about her, and I wanted to get to know her. I've already established that I wasn't into Punk at all, but if anyone could turn my head around, it was this compelling young woman. Keep in mind, this was a few years before the notorious anti-punk rock episode of Quincy would air, so at that time I was not under the influence of Dr. Quincy, a coroner whose detecting skills I couldn't help but respect.

But none of this meant she wasn't a suspect. What better way to build credibility in the punk community than by killing a prog-rock dinosaur?

She was reading a book of poems by Jim Carroll. As she turned a page, a loose-leaf page from a spiral notebook fell to the floor. I was right behind her, so I picked it up, thinking this might be a good opening for a conversation with her.

I glanced at the paper, and I saw that it was Red Herring's set-list. I hadn't been able to understand a single word of any of their lyrics, so this was my first glimpse into the content of Red Herring's songs.

I was startled by the song titles I saw:

"Kill Kill Kill Galactica Anathema"

"Brandon Penny Must Die"

"Electrocute All Synthesizer Scumbags"

"Prog Pukes Are Pigs"

"I Love You My Dearest Darling"

Okay, that last song title wasn't incriminating, but all the other ones sure were!

"Oh, my God!" I said, not realizing I was speaking out loud. "Red Herring killed Brandon Penny!"

The groupie turned and glared at me. She grabbed the piece of paper from my hand. "Mind your own business," she sneered. Then she shoved the paper in her mouth, quickly chewed, and swallowed it. I was grateful for those snacks I had had, otherwise I would have been envious of her having something to eat.

She went back to reading her book, ignoring me as if nothing had happened. I now knew that Red Herring were major suspects, maybe **the** major suspects, but I had no proof. The only way to get that set-list evidence from the groupie would be an autopsy from Quincy, and that would have made him anti-punk rock all over again.

Lieutenant Douglas, oblivious to the major break in the case that had just been digested, stood before us and launched into his spiel:

"It seems like this was a tragic accident, but as we continue to investigate, you might be contacted by some police and insurance people. I'm going to need all of your contact information.'

"I'll be contacting them!" Peter Payne announced. "I'm going to sue the Nassau Coliseum!"

"Whatever, fine," the Lieutenant responded. "All I'm telling you people is that once you give us your addresses and phone numbers, you can all go home."

There was a collective sigh of relief among everyone, but I was having none of it.

I stood up and said, "This was no accident!"

I was trying to make this point with my best Quincy emphasis, but I started to feel dizzy. Standing up so quickly had made the world around me seem like a TV that was getting bad reception.

"Shut your gob!" Peter Payne yelled. "This was no murder. It was an accident, the kind of accident that a business like this auditorium is completely liable for!"

"How convenient," I said. "Brandon Penny's death means an insurance and lawsuit payment windfall for you!"

He may have thought I was not prepared to deal with such issues, but murderous insurance scams had been of big part of many Mannix, Cannon, and Barnaby Jones episodes, so I had a lot of experience in this area. Hell, there was even a show called Longstreet where James Franciscus played a blind insurance investigator, but it was cancelled after only one season, so I guess Payne thought he could get away with this.

Since there were a lot of police around, I felt emboldened to confront Payne, even after he had threatened my life. But amazingly, Lieutenant Douglas was annoyed with me.

"This is none of your concern, hippie," he said. "Now everybody give me your contact information and go home."

It was time for me to drop the bomb.

"I guess you didn't know that Peter Payne paid the Ice Capades guy to drop the water on Brandon Penny," I said.

I expected a gasp, but everyone was bored and distracted and just wanted to go home. Then, surprisingly, it was the other surviving member of Galactica Anathema who dropped the real bomb:

"That's not true!" Noel Carson said, holding up his drumsticks for emphasis. "I'm the one who paid the Ice Capades guy, but he was supposed to drop the water on me, not Brandon."

This seemed very gasp-worthy, but once again, no one cared. I guess startling crime scene revelations are much more impactful when they happen before everyone is coming down from drugs.

"You paid him?" I said. I was shocked. Not as shocked as Brandon Penny was when he was electrocuted to death, but shocked nonetheless.

"It was supposed to happen in the middle of my drum solo," Carson said. "I thought it would be a really cool effect, and I was far enough away from any electronic equipment, so I would be safe from being electrocuted to death. But this bloody idiot from the Ice Capades jumped his cue and killed Brandon."

"No, no, it's not true!" the Ice Capades guy screamed. "I didn't do it. I wasn't backstage when it happened. I meant to come around later when Noel Carson's drum solo was scheduled to happen. That was in the next song.

This was true. The song being played when the water dropped was a showcase for Brandon Penny's playing, and that song, their most successful single, still had at least another forty-five minutes to go.

But there was still a glaring problem with his story, and I was the only one aware of it:

"Then why did Peter Payne pay you," I said. "I saw the whole transaction."

"I handle all the finances of the band," Payne said. "Carson ran the water idea by me, but we didn't have anything in the budget for a new special effect. This tour is bleeding money. So he paid for it out of his own pocket. He gave the money to me and I gave the money to the Ice Capades guy."

"I have a name, you know!" the Ice Capades guy screamed. But he didn't use this opportunity to remind us of it, he had a more important thing to say: "I'm not the one who dropped with water! It was not my fault!"

And then, as if he hadn't incriminated himself enough already, he turned and ran. I knew this was the exact moment for a frantic chase with the killer, the kind I had seen a million times on Mannix, but when I stood up again, I got another intense dizzying rush, so I sat back down and hoped maybe I could stop him with telekineses. Yes, I was high enough for such a thought, but also rational enough to know it was a nonstarter.

But the Ice Capades guy didn't get far because he tripped over the mellotron that was still on the floor.

"That's my retirement fund you just tripped over you bloody fool," the roadie yelled, but the mellotron wasn't damaged. Those things were built to endure both mood-inducing keyboard fantasias, and fleeing murderer suspects.

Lieutenant Douglas picked the Ice Capades guy up off the floor and was about to arrest and book him, I assumed, but then Lisa spoke up.

"Hey, I can vouch for him," she said. "I was in a conference room with him discussing logistics for the Ice Capades load-in tomorrow. There were plenty of witnesses because there were other arena staff members there as well. The meeting was interrupted by the commotion of the accident. So he couldn't have possibly been backstage when the water fell."

"I told you all, I was planning to be there for the next song," the Ice Capades guy said. "Someone else dumped that water on Brandon Penny."

"Or, more likely, it happened accidentally," Peter Payne said, visions of lawsuit and insurance money dancing in his head. "The water that the Ice Capades guy left in the rafters fell over when it wasn't supposed to, and an accidental albeit easily preventable tragedy happened. End of story."

No, not end of story. Not by a long shot. But I was the only one who felt this way.

I sat down. I was disheartened.

"Hey, don't feel bad, dude," Jim said. "We've got tickets to see King Crimson next month. Maybe a more solvable murder will happen there."

"Thanks, but Robert Fripp doesn't have to die to make me feel better," I said.

Jim, Becky and I got up to leave. I was ready to file the whole evening as a cold case that I might not be able to solve.

I was in a dark mood.

Then, my mind was blown.

Over the arena's sound system, the Ice Capades organist began playing — I couldn't believe it — the theme from Mannix!

"This is amazing!" I said, my spirits instantly lifted. "I've got to go talk some Mannix with the organist."

"Crappy commercial pap!" Jim said dismissively.

Jim was too much of a snob to appreciate the musical genius of Lalo Schifrin (he wrote not just the Mannix theme, but also the Mission Impossible theme, I mean, come on!). I told Becky and Jim I'd only be a minute and meet them outside, then I headed over to the booth where the organ was.

When I arrived there, the lady organist was playing the Mannix theme with great dexterity, which was doubly impressive considering her age.

The music came to its conclusion, right around the point where the "Wardrobe furnished by Botany 500" credit would have been.

I gave her a sincere round of applause. I realized that when a person is clapping by themselves it can come off as sarcastic, but I was being genuine and I think she sensed that.

"Why thank you, young man," she said. "I wouldn't expect a hippie like you to appreciate good music."

"I love the Mannix theme," I said. "Also the themes of Cannon, Streets of San Francisco, Emergency, Adam 12 and Barnaby Jones."

She started playing the Barnaby Jones theme and it sounded so good I wished I was higher so I could enjoy it even more.

"So, you like Barnaby Jones, too?" I said.

"Oh, dear, yes," she replied. "I was the one who came up with the idea for the 'Barnaby Jones on Ice' show."

"Wait, there was a Barnaby Jones on Ice show?" I said. "How did I miss that?"

"Oh, it was a big hit. It played at Madison Square Garden right before 'Mannix-Capades', also a huge success."

I was confused. I hadn't heard of either of these shows and if anyone was in the target audience, it was me. How did they escape my notice?

"And the 'Delvecchio Follies' did even better," she said. "I was the organist at every show."

Okay, now she was coming off as delusional. Something didn't add up. Sure, Barnaby Jones on Ice and Mannix-Capades were both plausible, even though I had never heard of them. I mean, who wouldn't go to these show if they were properly publicized? (Obviously they weren't.)

But the Delvecchio Follies? No way! Delvecchio was a detective show starring Judd Hirsch. It was barely on the air for one season. Who in their right mind would turn that into an arena ice show?

Well, I thought, she might not be in her right mind but at least she was sweet.

"It's nice to meet a young man who isn't a fan of the kind of vulgar, loud, awful music that was played tonight," she said.

"Actually, I was here to see the show."

"Blaspheming satanist!" she screamed, abruptly turning on me.

Then she laughed maniacally. "Well, at least no one will have to hear that crappy keyboard player anymore."

There was a searing hatred in her voice as she continued: "All of today's rock music, it's so bad. A good musician, a true musician like yours truly, is relegated to playing ice skating rinks and baseball games. It's not fair!"

"Okay, I'm going to ask you something," I said. "And for your own good, and for the good of your conscience, you need to give me an honest answer."

And then I bluntly hit her with the question that simply had to be asked: "Was there really a Delvecchio Follies?"

"I am the dream weaver!" she replied, her eyes becoming more crazed as she spoke. "I am the weaver of dreams. I can make them happen, whether it's Barnaby Jones on Ice, or Mannix-Capades, or whatever a heart desires. What is it you want? An immersive avant-garde production of Please Don't Eat the Daisies? For a price I can conjure anything. Except, apparently, the spectacular music career that I so richly deserve!"

Wait a minute, I thought, I might be dealing with a psycho here. And psychos can be murderers, at least the ones capable of multitasking. But mental instability wasn't enough to implicate her in Brandon Penny's death. I needed evidence.

She smiled, maybe to seem less crazed, but her open mouth revealed that her teeth contained Brandon Penny's famous keyboard dentures. The groupie had said that a member of the band's stage crew had taken them, and I noticed one of those Nassau Coliseum crew jumpsuits hanging up on the wall next to the organ, along with a Galactica Anathema baseball cap, both of which the groupie said the so-called crew member wore when "he" took the dentures. The old lady's grey hair was cropped short; seen from behind with the cap and jumpsuit on, it would be easy to mistake her for a male crew member.

This was interesting and all, but what I needed was some kind of evidence.

Then, on top of the organ I saw an envelope with the "Ice Capades" logo on it. It had the same blueberry snow cone stain I had noticed earlier on the envelope that had been used to make the payment to have the water dropped on Brandon

Penny. So the Ice Capades guy had put the money Peter Payne gave him into the envelope, and then he had given the envelope stuffed with money to this nice old lady, because in her delusional state, she had convinced him that for a fee she could make his dreams of an immersive avant-garde dinner theater production of Please Don't Eat The Daises come true.

Damn, if only I had some evidence!

Next to the envelope was a discarded Crunchie candy wrapper, which could only be obtained in England, except for the ones taken to America by Brian Seaford, who had given one to Brandon Penny, and then had been removed from Penny's dead body, but only by someone who would have been there shortly after he died. Amid all the chaos, the same person dressed as a crew member could have removed the candy at the same time "he" removed the dentures.

Just one piece of evidence was all I needed.

Next to the candy wrapper was a big green magic marker, exactly the kind that had been used by Brandon Penny to sign the mellotron. The roadie said the magic marker was lent to him by a Nassau Coliseum crew member, and both the magic marker and the coliseum uniform were clearly visible right now before my very eyes.

But I wasn't even thinking about that. I was thinking about how much I needed to find some evidence to support my suspicion.

And then I noticed that the Nassau Coliseum jumpsuit hanging on her wall was stained with grime and dirt on the pants part, especially around the knees. It was exactly the kind of stain you would get from crawling along a cat walk above a stage to drop a bucket of water on a musician.

Unfortunately, I had nothing to go on, so now my only recourse was to wildly accuse her of something I had no proof of.

"The 'Barnaby Jones on Ice,' 'Mannix-Capades' and 'Delvecchio Follies' never happened, did they?" I said. "You made them all up. You monster!'"

She just shook her head. "Kids these days," she muttered under her breath.

"The Ice Capades guy told you about the plan to drop water on the drummer during the show," I continued. "He told you that's how he was going to get the money to pay you for the Please Don't Eat the Daisies production you said you could make happen for him, bogusly I might add. You knew he would be busy with the production meeting and that's when you dressed as a Nassau Coliseum crew member and went backstage yourself and intentionally dropped the water on Brandon Perry to intentionally kill him."

She glanced around the room, then let out a laugh, which managed to sound sweet and depraved at the same time.

"I had just noticed that all of this stuff here could be construed as incriminating evidence," she said. "So to make sure that no one came in here, I started playing the Mannix theme, because I figured that would make all you freaked-out hippies stay away from here. But it was like a siren call to you, wasn't it? My, you are a strange young man."

"You really did kill Brandon Penny, didn't you?" I said.

"So what?" she replied "I was ridding the world of one more flashy overrated musician, the kind that makes the world more difficult for someone like me, an artist who in a past era was on her way to a successful career, until rock music came along and ruined everything, destroying my dreams. He and every rock keyboardist deserves to die!"

She said this forcefully, but I was a bit distracted because I suddenly remembered that the set list the groupie had eaten would have proven beyond a doubt that Red Herring had killed Brandon Penny, and it was such a shame that I didn't have that evidence, and all I had here was this woman's confession.

Wait, what? Confession?

I tried to gather my thoughts, which was not an easy task under any circumstance, but before I could, she stood up, grabbed the back of my neck, and slammed my head up against the concrete wall.

For most of the night, I had smoked so much pot and drank so much beer that I was frequently hovering in and out of unconsciousness, but this time I didn't need drugs to pass out, my near-coma concussion happened naturally and organically.

When I came to, Becky and Jim were crouched over me.

"Dude, wake up," Jim was saying.

"Come on, it's time to go home," Becky said.

I was disoriented. It took me a moment to regain my usual state of sleep walking.

Then I remembered.

"The organist!" I cried out. "She did this to me!"

"Yeah, right," Jim said, laughing.

"Come on," Becky said. "You're so wasted you banged into the wall. I saw that sweet old lady leave the arena a few moments ago. Let's go home."

The organist had taken all the evidence with her, although at that moment I couldn't quite remember what it was. I wanted to find that old lady and have a high-speed chase with her, but I was still a couple weeks away from taking my drivers ed test.

We went home.

The next day I was all ready to get working on the case and prove that this sweet organist lady had killed Brandon Penny. I smoked a joint, then looked at the TV guide to double check that Rockford Files wasn't preempted that week. Once I had that figured out, I stood up, and then I sat back down, because my head was still hurting from the blow it had taken the previous night.

I opened the newspaper, and the headline on the front page of Newsday jolted me:

MULTIPLE BODIES FOUND BURIED IN BACKYARD OF WESTBURY MUSIC TEACHER.

You've all heard of her. Jannie Jenkins. She became known as the Westbury Body Burier. And she was none other than the same organist lady I had encountered the previous evening.

All of the bodies found were young guys, around my age, who had come to her for music lessons. They all aspired to be keyboardists in rock bands, and she hated modern rock music so much that she killed them all and then buried their bodies in her backyard.

When I saw the pictures of her victims, I was particularly struck by the way they looked. One kid resembled Rick Wakeman, the keyboardist of Yes, another was the spitting image of Keith Emerson, of Emerson, Lake and Palmer. The remaining kids looked similar to Stevie Winwood, Tony Banks and other prog or prog-adjacent musicians.

She obviously had a psychotic, obsessive hatred of prog organists, and the physical similarities of the kids triggered her. And then when she had the chance to kill Brandon Penny, who was playing at an arena she had access to as a freelance Ice Capades employee, she leapt at the chance to murder him. It all made perfect sense.

To me, not to anyone else. I took my theory to Lieutenant Douglas, who was her arresting officer. When I told him it was all part of a pattern, he told me to get lost or he'd book me for public intoxication, which was a bogus charge, although I was too high to know if he was bluffing or not.

He told me the incident at the Nassau Coliseum had been declared an accident, and I was being a pest. I figured this case was a dead end, but it didn't matter, there would be plenty of other cases and plenty of time for me to solve them.

Only I never came across anything like this again. The Westbury Body Burier has become an iconic grizzly true crime case with several books, documentaries, movies, and TV mini-series about it.

It was especially galling to me when Mannix himself, Mike Connors, played Lieutenant Douglas in a TV movie about the case. I knew for a fact that the Lieutenant had never watched a single episode of Mannix. I would have liked to have gone to the set of the movie and told Mike Connors about this personally, but guess what? It wasn't filmed on Long Island, it was filmed in Burbank, CA. It's almost as if television and reality are two completely different things.

EPILOGUE
"THE LAMB LIES DOWN ON MURDER"

Not long after this all went down, I started to realize that my skills as a detective were lacking in certain respects. Even my theory about Red Herring being the murderers, which seemed iron-clad, didn't quite pan out. Yes, they had written lyrics on the spur of the moment about how much they hated Galactica Anathema and wanted them dead, but I later found out they did that for every band they opened for. It was just a punk attitude kind of thing. They even had a minor hit a year or so later with "I'd Like To Bash Your Skull, Jethro Tull."

I stayed a druggie for a few more years. I was too out of it to go to college, and I ended up working a series of menial go-nowhere jobs. It's hard to become a crime fighter when you're a Taco Bell employee. The one time a robbery happened there, I was folding tortilla shells in the back kitchen and I missed the whole thing. But by that time I didn't much care anymore.

It began to dawn on me that I was a loser. Well, that's not completely true, it would be more accurate to say I was a total loser.

So I stopped smoking pot, drinking booze, and taking drugs. I started going to AA meetings.

I got a job as a night watchman, and I was pretty good at it, mainly because I met the one requirement for the gig: I didn't fall asleep. For someone who used to frequently fall into a drug and beer-induced slumber in the middle of the afternoon, this was quite a personal evolution.

I got a reputation in the building I worked in for being dependable, and the building management company promoted me to an office job where I supervised other night watchmen and security guards, and took care of various other responsibilities.

It wasn't exactly an exciting career, but through my twelve step meetings and friendships, I learned to have self-respect, and at one of the meetings I met a woman who looked familiar, and we got together for coffee. She invited me to a party where she and a bunch of friends watched the anti-punk rock Quincy episode and made fun of it. That's when I realized she was the Red Herring groupie who had eaten the evidence all those years earlier.

She still loved punk (just like I still love prog) and when I got to know her better, I found out she ran a Columbo fan site, and we spent hours talking about our favorite 1970s crime shows. We've been going together ever since. I haven't revealed her name, or my name, for that matter, in order to maintain our anonymity in the program. She's a little more up on the modern world than I am, so she's the one who told me about the true crime podcast craze.

So now I'm doing this true crime podcast about the Westbury Body Burier. I know there have already been lots of podcasts and documentaries and books about this very subject. But nobody has ever known the never-before-heard details I'm giving you now, about the truth of this crime: Brandon Penny's death was no accident, it was murder, and Jannie Jenkins, the notorious Westbury Body Burier, did it!

And I can exclusively bring you these new facts, thanks to my sober way of life and my clear-headed mind. When I look back on how I behaved in the 1970s, I'm relieved and grateful that I'm no longer the neglectful, foggy brained dim bulb I used to be. And as I sit here, talking into my iPhone, and looking at the screen, which I once found so technologically daunting, I'm happy to finally be a part of the modern…

Wait a minute.

Crap.

I probably should have pushed the record button.